G

'Have you no
husband recently?' asked

Peggy turned from him, blushing: 'It's slightly embarrassing. He walked out of his spaceship and just took me on the heather. He didn't even say "hello". And I had the most peculiar feeling – when he was making love to me. One of his hands was pulling away at my flying suit, while another toyed with a nipple. And, I know it sounds impossible, but I was sure I felt *a third hand between my legs . . .*'

Also by Fiona Richmond in *Star*

FIONA
THE STORY OF I
ON THE ROAD
THE GOOD, THE BAD, AND THE BEAUTIFUL

GALACTIC GIRL

Fiona Richmond

A STAR BOOK

published by
the Paperback Division of
W. H. ALLEN & Co. Ltd

A Star Book
Published in 1980
by the Paperback Division of
W. H. Allen & Co. Ltd
A Howard and Wyndham Company
44 Hill Street, London W1X 8LB

Printed in Great Britain by
Hunt Barnard Printing Ltd., Aylesbury, Bucks.

ISBN 0 352 30747 1

To Ralph, Richard, Andrew, John, Adrian, Eddie, Ray, Steve and Simon. May they keep coming (for a Burton) again and again! !

CONTENTS

CHAPTER ONE

Unidentified Flying Person

Engines raced, vibrating the whole body of the monster.

Peggy Sue edged towards the open door. The wind whipped viciously around her slender form. She arrived at the very edge of the precipice. Her toes curled in her boots. She nervously tapped the toe of one steel stiletto against the edge of the open portal. Reaching out, she grabbed the metal grips at the side of the door, preparing for her launch into the yawning void. She didn't mean to look down. Too late. Way below, she could see the patchwork quilt of matchbox-sized fields. She felt a hand press firmly into her back. For a brief moment she resisted its pressure. Then she jumped.

She could feel nothing; she could see nothing. Coming out of her disorientated state, she took up the usual free-fall position, stretching her arms and legs wide in an X-shape. Now, she could see the ground mapped out beneath her. There was little sensation of falling – no feeling that the ground was getting closer. Peggy luxuriated in the silent peace of her weightlessness. She glanced at her wrist altimeter and saw that she was now at three and a half thousand feet. Time to pull the chute. The handle moved and Peggy waited five seconds. She glanced up to where the silk mushroom should have been . . .

Failure. Panic. Her heart thudded uncomfortably in her breast. Her chute had failed. No time to lose. She dragged the handle from the reserve pack on her chest. She dived a hand into the tightly-packed bag, cupping the folds of material into her palm. And prayed. In those brief seconds, her life flashed before her. Very badly edited! Then, with one almighty heave, she threw the reserve pack from her, as far as she could. The life-saving silk spread out above her. In the nick of time . . . Her shoulders strained as the lines pulled tight and her descent slowed to a more comfortable pace. The world took on more normal proportions. She began to breathe more easily. The horizons seemed to move rapidly away from her, as the ground rushed up to meet her. At about fifty feet, she took the customary crouched foetal position and waited for the impact.

She landed on the soft mattress of heather. She was thinking of his coming. And her own . . .

She reclined on a thick purple carpet on a black granite outcrop. The glen swept down to the ice-cold waters of Lock McCock. Rising from the centre of the smooth unbroken water's surface was an island. Atop this small isle snuggled a wee white croftie. Smoke curled gracefully from the brick chimney stack. There was a welcome in the glen.

Meanwhile, up above, Peggy's mind was light years away from this peaceful pastoral scene. Rockets, robots and rods were the stuff of her thinking. Her brain locked into thoughts of erotics. Tom. Tom's dick was hairy. And so was the rest of him. Soft, black hair covered his athletic masculine frame. His powerful neck supported a finely-chiselled head. His was the face that had launched a thousand spaceships. His head was covered with a thick thatch of ebony curls. And there was much power between his legs. Peggy thought longingly of the fat sexual slug that lay curled in a beautiful birds-nest in the crook of his thighs. All she need do was offer a little flash of her fan, for it to be transformed into a throbbing thrusty tapir's tongue. A miniature tidal wave of sex seepings saturated the silken web of lace at her crotch. She closed her eyes and laid herself open to the heat which now consumed her pussy.

As one of her hands disappeared under the rim of her knicks, the visual calm of the scene was shattered by a stream of colour which slashed the sky.

Its end settled neatly between her thrashing thighs. Tom obsessed her racing thoughts, as the seven-hued phallus possessed her. To the casual Mactavish, who was roaming through that particular gloamin', it appeared that Peggy was opening up to receive the multi-coloured cock. She rose to meet the shaft of indigo, violet, red, orange, yellow, green and blue. She spread her legs wide and squirmed under the rock-hard Blackpool illumination. It was a rainbow fuck; and her cunt, the crock of gold at its end.

Suddenly a wind got up. The aforementioned casual Mactavish farted into his kilt! The Mistral, slow at first, lapped around Peggy's waiting pudenda and caressed her near-naked body. Peggy had unzipped her one-piece second-skin silver flying suit. Her spent parachute lay in folds on the ground behind her. Gusts of wind playfully rippled the silk and teased at her shining coverall – which wasn't covering much! As her movements got more frantic, the wind whistled. The heather opened up like the crack in your bum. Bushes bowed under the force of the whirlwind. Trees cowed. She was so engrossed in her lather of passion that she didn't notice the space module land, but a few feet from her writhing form. The circular steel vehicle settled without a bump among the bracken. The bright red lights which surrounded its rim winked and blinked like a weird species of Peeping Tom. The quiet drone of its V54 engines died away. The wind dropped to a whisper; just as quickly as Peggy had come. Majestic calm descended on the gloamin'.

The eerie stillness was fractured by a high pitch whine,

coming from the very bowels of the strange UFO. But Peggy, still unseeing, was in the last throes of her space-shattering orgasm. The flying machine split around its middle and opened like an oyster. Out stepped a pearl. The unidentified flying person made an awesome spectacle, silhouetted against the brilliant blue sky. He drank in the view. Peggy's wide-open crotch magnetised his eyes; as did the many-shaded shaft that penetrated her privates. His gaze travelled the length and breadth of her silver-coated body. From the top of her erotic head, over the tips of her erotic tits, to the tips of her erotic toes. Pencil-thin stiletto-heeled boots covered her dainty feet. A suggestion of scarlet peeped from the open-toed front of each silver shoe. The high backs were turned down in an elegant pleat. Above them, the metallic material was moulded to every line of the girl's legs. He perceived the gentle curves of her calves and the long, lissom lines of her thighs. They seemed to go on forever (like this bleeding description . . .). Her legs lead wonderfully to wide-open delights. Her suit had fallen away from her secret parts. The ingenious piece of clothing had a double zip which allowed her to open front and back and expose her body in its entirety (except for the elbows). The lace of her knickers was wet and transparent. The UFP could make out the moist pink lips of her pussy which were trying to break free of the confining net of her panties. The rosebud was topped by a field of wild grass. Her pubic patch glinted and sparkled in the bright light. The fair curls lay so neatly on her pubic pinnacle, they seemed to have been tongued into place. Her taut, tanned tummy was bare. Her neat navel was furled and as seductive as a mini-clit. The swell of her hips swooped in to a tiny waist. Her hands half-covered her bountiful breasts. Her dewy, brown nipples peeped cheekily from between her fingers. Her head was flung back in an orgasmic gesture. Her full pink lips were parted slightly. The last dying sounds of her climax rumbled at the back of her deep throat. A hiss of escaping breath rasped through her white teeth. Wisps of golden hair framed the peachy skin of her visage.

The stranger broke from his reverie and strode purposefully towards her. Lead-lined boots hit the heather with a thud. The creature appeared to be at least eight foot tall. He strongly resembled a larger-than-life Michelin Man. His cock defied gravity within his suit. Its bucking buckled the fabric.

Peggy, realising something was afoot, sat up and saw that it was in fact feet. Two huge ones – which came to rest but a foreskin's breadth from her nose. Her gaze travelled on and up the towering mobile lighthouse. His piercing green eyes bore into her skull and she shivered. Her heart pounded, her pulse raced and her quim quivered. There was menace in the space-being's eyes . . .

In a spaceship three miles left of Mars, Fatman and Robinski were up to no good – as usual. They paced up and down the control deck, slapping their fists into their palms and saying 'Gosh' a lot. Robinski pulled her forelock a lot too.

'Gee whiz, Fatman, the Russians' plan to take over the earth and turn it into another intergalactic brothel in their chain, sure is a devilish one. But I wish you'd tell me *your* plan.'

'Not yet, Robinski. Not until I've got everything under control. Navek could still cause us trouble, though. I think he'll have to use all his intellectuals to stop us now.'

An evil glint came into Fatman's pink eyes as he surveyed the bank of knobs and lights at the hub of their interplanetary cruiser. He eyed the sophisticated controls with pride; puffing up like a stuffed turkey. He'd done so well for himself! His mother would be proud of him! Here he was, a simple lad from Wigan, masterminding the most fiendish plot ever to hit the Universe.

Peggy returned her husband's gaze. Love leaked from the green eyes of the recently-returned astronaut. She'd not been expecting his descent so soon . . . nor hers. He'd brought her abruptly back to earth from an amazing orgasmic orbit. She watched as her man struggled with the buckles and straps of his vast pressurised overall. It blew off and sailed up into the blue yonder, like a large white elephant in flight. A passing head clansman, thinking it was some new species of grouse, peppered it with shot and the white inflatable, giving up the ghost, executed a sloppy landing into the loch. Naked, apart from his fetching lead-weighted boots, Tom bent to kiss her. A shiver ran through her body as his lips met hers through the feather-light gossamer of her knickers. His tongue flicked over the disturbed (very) curly mass of her pubes. While one hand eased the lace material from her patch and pulled the last vestiges of her flying suit from her inert body, another worked away at her nipples, bringing them quickly to pointing perfection, and yet another laboured at her labia. Somewhat alarmed by this inhuman turn of events, she looked quickly down to check out the octopus below.

Nothing.

'Must have been my over-active imagination,' she thought.

Her body ached to be violated by his strong steel shaft. It had been three weeks or more since she'd tasted his sex. In another instant, the two naked shapes were locked in a panting passionate embrace. Tom held Peggy to his heaving breast and played a welcome tattoo with his fingertips on her breasts. He pulled her face to his and his tongue darted into her mouth. The probes melted in a long-awaited kiss.

From a hidden vantage point, not more than a hundred yards away, Navek Mactavish watched the scene of love. His expression was grim; his jaw clamped tight. His eyes took in every detail, every nuance, of the couple's love-making. He was powerless to stop the lovers. But his time would come. And so would he!

Tom withdrew his tongue from Peggy's mouth and began a southbound migration. His lips travelled over her creamy neck and swiftly moved down; down to her magnificent breasts. His lips gently sucked in a nipple and his tongue teased at its tip. It became as hard as a nut under his loving ministrations. He moved on and dipped down over the smooth slope that led to Peggy's navel. His tongue played around the passion cleft, causing the woman beneath him to moan in pleasure. His mouth caressed the very edge of Peggy's silken curls and then plunged into the lubricated well between her legs. He'd eased his body around and, with eyes closed, Peggy became aware that his long pulsing loofah was begging for attention as it bounced on her cheek. She opened her mouth, moved her head fractionally and tongued the end of his powerful manhood. It jerked its approval. Her lips closed over the knob and Tom's body shuddered as he felt the first movements of his come at the base of his balls. His tongue moved wildly in her slot as he savoured her special love cocktail. She licked at his shaft, as it bucked and throbbed on its countdown to ecstasy. He could feel his jissome being forced along its fucking path. But he didn't want to spill his seed yet. This load had its future already mapped out. It would water his lady's garden of delights and he would not loose it, except in that delight-filled hole. He moved away from her pussy and eased himself around until they were again face-to-face, crotch-to-crotch.

His hard threepiece suite squashed against her hair-fringed-minge. Peggy lay there thinking that, for an astronaut, his aim wasn't up to much. She giggled inwardly at her jest but forgave him immediately, because four weeks without oats makes for a wobbly aim! He righted his wrong and shafted her like a hot knife might slip through butter. Her sweet sex doughnut creamed as she gobbled him in. He dunked his wick in her sugar-coated slot and she gasped at his violent attack upon her person. Sugar turned to honey. Peggy became weightless.

Waves of climactic cock-shudders told her he was on the point of bursting his sperm banks. She felt the drip drip of his juice turn into a geyser, as he blasted off within her. She clawed at his back. He ground her into the earth. She pulled him down, attempting to drag him into her inner orbit. Seconds later, she took the path to the Land of Climaxes. The lovers lay still in their warm heather cocoon.

She glanced upward at the sweet face of her man and drank in his perfect profile. With eyes closed, jaw slack and his entire body so obviously at peace, she realised how much she loved this strong man from the skies.

But she suddenly had the strangest feeling that they were being watched. She looked to her left and could see nothing but a thick verdant clump of bracken. As she watched, the ferns parted and she found herself staring into two piercing violet eyes.

Peggy screamed and gesticulated wildly in the direction of the moving greenery. Tom slipped out of her and leapt to his feet. In two manly strides, he was upon the foe in the foliage. With a blinding flash, the enemy disappeared.

'Nothing there,' said Tom.

'But there was,' insisted Peggy. 'I definitely saw two eyes staring at us out of the gloom.'

'You must have been imagining it.'

'What was that flash then?'

'Just a little bit of freak lightning, dear.'

'Some freak, darling,' said Peggy impatiently. 'I definitely heard the unmistakable rustle of a Scotsman's kilt. And a squeak of bagpipe. And just look at that haggis lying on its pile of neeps. How do you think that got there?'

'The remains of some local's picnic. Just a coincidence darling. Nothing to worry about.'

'But I *am* worried. Something very odd is going on around here. You've been away for a month. While you were gone, I've been aware of a feeling of always being watched. Every time I lie out on the patio, I catch sight of the glint of binoculars across the loch on the mainland. And I'm sure they're always trained on me.'

'There's nothing unusual about that,' soothed Tom. 'If you must sunbathe in the nude, you should expect some interest in your rudeness.'

'No, Tom, I'm sure there's something more to it than that. They're still there watching me, when I row across the loch to go to the village to buy provisions. And I'll tell you something else, when I've been getting my oats for the porridge from the store – you know, Mrs Linley – well, there's always a Scotsman in a kilt leaning against a lamp-post outside. And he reads his newspaper upside down. I've not seen his face but the knees are unmistakably the same.'

'I didn't know you were such an expert on knees. And the newspaper thing – he probably had *Men Only* tucked inside. Don't you worry your little brain about this, dear. I'm sure there's a simple explanation. Now gird up your loins, your flying suit, your parachute, and we'll go home. I'll just chain up my space module. I don't want anyone fiddling with my flying saucer!'

Tom executed this laborious task with speed and verve – which was only to be expected of this fine figure of an athletic man. Linking hands, the lovers ran down the grassy slope to the water's edge. The loch lapped against the shore. Flinging their flying suits aside and discarding their footwear, the two plunged recklessly into the inviting water. Their squeals of delight turned to shrieks of horror, as the glacial waters enveloped them. Tom's balls shot up into his body and Peggy's pudenda froze rigid. Icicles hung daintily from her pubes.

With great perspicacity, Tom cried: 'Gosh this water's cold. Let's get home, Peglet. Look – blue tits.'

'Where?' replied his wife, looking upward for a passing cloud of birds.

Nothing to be seen though. She quickly realised it was her very cold mammaries to which he jokingly referred. The two rushed from the icy clutches of the H_20 and dashed up the beach to their boathouse. Tom flung open the doors and leapt into their extra-long Cadillac. Peggy jumped in beside him and the motor roared as Tom accelerated down the beach and into the water. Happily, the car was amphibious and beetled easily across the loch.

The gleaming machine left the water and came to rest – dripping seaweed and all manner of marine life, the odd limpet and the strange barnacle – outside the front door of their picturesque island hideaway. The staff was lined up outside; on the gravel forecourt which led to the rose-infested front door. The staff consisted of a person of unspecified sex. It was wearing a skirt, however, and it bobbed a curtsey. So, it was probably female. But you can never tell in Scotland, can you?

A voice like a foghorn (very useful when the mists roll down) said: 'Welcome to McCock.'

'I didn't think you'd have one,' said Tom, wondering why his wife had employed a transvestite during his absence.

'Good evening,' said Tom, breezily slapping her around the head to show her who was boss!

The new maid, Ms Tree, turned the other cheek, so Tom hit that too.

Peggy, somewhat taken aback by this unexpected fisticuffs, said: 'That's not very friendly, Tom,' and hustled them all inside to safety.

She had been quite impressed with the nonchalent way

the new home-help, Violet, had coped with their strange arrival, dripping and naked and covered in seaweed. But was a little perturbed at the brutality shown by Tom. Things were getting stranger and stranger. She couldn't think what had got into her husband. He was normally so placid and mild-mannered. It suddenly occurred to her that he'd recently ravished her without even saying 'hello'. And now he was mistreating the servants . . .

Peggy had become quite fond of Violet over the time that Tom had been away. She put down the latter's weird behaviour to his space travelling. After all, he had a lot of responsibility as commander of Milky Way, the space station with the less fattening centre. At 30, he was the youngest Major in the entire space fleet. With nerves of steel, or some such similar hard metal, he was exceptionally well suited to his role.

The firelight flickered on their faces as they relaxed in front of the cozy glow. Peggy had on a robe of peach silk – almost the same colour as her skin. It had fallen open enabling Tom to contemplate her thighs and magnificent mound. Long, smooth, creamy legs crossed carelessly one over the other. Her golden hair fell across her face in a heavy veil. He could just make out one blue sparking eye, which peeped mischievously through the cobweb of her spun silk hair. Tom reached out and caught her chin in his hand. He tilted it up and her hair cascaded in a waterfall from her face. Her glossy lips pouted petulantly; then parted in a knowing smile. The eyes danced, glancing boldly down between Tom's legs, where the tell-tale flagpole raised his robe in a salacious salute.

Ms Tree had gone to bed, after serving them an excellent cold supper of grouse, tossed salad, which she'd shot herself, and a particularly good bottle of Chateau McCock '69. Tom had visibly relaxed, and Peggy was pleased to see the return of her husband's old self. They lay together in a clinch on the hearthrug. Peggy was just thinking how peaceful was the night, when Tom gave her a legover. His hands eased the fine material of her robe from her shoulders. He tugged at the cord which circled her waist. The gown fell completely away, revealing her naked beauty in its entirety. He lifted Peggy's body gently from the carpet and slipped the garment from her. He tossed it casually to one side and Peggy began her assault on his short toga. She unravelled the tasselled cord and parted the towelling material. The unveiling ceremony complete, she took the ornate tassel and dangled it on the tip of his cock. The feathers of rope brushed gently against his pounding knob. He grabbed her roughly in his arms and pinioned her to the short and curlies of the carpet. The rough broadloom prickled her back. His hard cock tickled her front. She felt as if she was surrounded by a hirsute womb; shag below and shag above. She loved her man's hairiness. She loved to run her fingers over the soft down of his chest; and to dally in the furry cleft of his buttocks. Tom ran his hands up and down the length of Peggy's body. He drew away and began licking down the tingling flesh of her inner thigh until he came to rest in her valley of delights. His gateway to cockdom. She loved to watch his dark head busying itself between her thighs. His tongue entered her dark warm hollow and his lips nibbled gently at her clitty; a soft-centred Dairy Box chocolate. While he was burrowing there, his hands crept up and slid over the pliant flesh of her buttocks. He kneaded her doughiness and cupped each cheek in a palm. He lifted the marshmallow orbs and pressed his face hard into her. She could feel his nose ferreting in her fur. His tongue was doing indescribable things, as it inched its way down her warm well. Peggy felt the first tremor of wonderment in her honeypot, as the heat of his tongue spread a warm glow through her womb. Her lust rose to fever pitch. Sensing an imminent explosion of passion, Tom drew his head away. Peggy slid down under him and Tom's cock cast an awe-some shadow upon her face. She fastened her eager hands around his beauteous bulge. It grew with every movement of her deft digits.

'I'm going to make myself come by rubbing the smooth tip of your cock against my pussy,' Peggy informed.

Tom's eyes widened with desire as his wife positioned herself astride his body. His cock waved heavenward as she jiggled herself into position. She didn't look down, not once; she felt her way through the entire manoeuvre, with her eyes fixed on his sex-crazed stare. Taking a firm grip on his shaft, she steered it towards her manhole. Contact. With light strokes, she covered her lips with cock kisses. She used the weapon to pleasure herself. The beast, however, seemed to have a will of its own and its head kept diving for her muff.

'No, you don't my boy,' she said nicely. 'You're my captive, my prisoner. Don't struggle. It's no use. I'm going to use your knob. I'm going to stroke it up and down between my legs until I come. But I'm not going to let you into my pussy. And you're not going to like that, are you?'

Peggy's eyes glazed as she worked his pecker like a piston, her juices oiled its head as it slipped and slithered among the velvety folds. Tom was desperate to bathe in her bidet. If she didn't let him soon, it would be too late. Her vice-like grip on his tool became even tighter as she humped her way to heaven. She went rigid; her breathing stopped and her eyes closed. Shudders coursed through her elegant form as she rocketed into outer space. She bathed his cock in a torrent of her sex sauces. It became too much for him. His sperm gush began. He watched fascinated as the pearly liquid pumped like a fountain. The milky substance shot straight as an arrow, bang on target.

Bullseye!

CHAPTER TWO

A 'Mole' in the Hole

Robinski looked in horror as her boss stroke lover stroke anything ran amok in his drab, grey-walled, Moscow office. The slim, petite, Mongolian girl crouched in a corner and ducked the missiles that Fatman, with great nonchalance, hurled over his shoulder. He grabbed at the pictures on the walls, ground them underfoot and wrenched the flimsy curtains from their hangings at the window. He pulled out the drawers of his desk and turned the contents out on to the floor. He yanked open the heavy drawers of the filing cabinet and paper confettied all over the room. The carpet was the next object of his assault. Starting at one corner, he pulled the threadbare rug from the floor and tugged it towards him. Unfortunately, Robinski was standing on the other end. As Fatman executed his bizarre tablecloth trick, Robinski fell flat on her back. She thought this an opportune moment to ask what the fuck he was doing.

'I've got it,' he mimed.

'Well, don't give it to me,' shrilled the Mongolian joker from her supine position upon the rough Russian boards. 'But what have you got?' she added mystified.

Excitedly, he waved his short fat arms in the air and

pointed to the centre of the floor, where lay a large brass plate fastened by four big screws. He raised a plump finger to his fat lips and motioned his sidekick to be silent. He waddled across to her, pursed his lips in her ear and whispered. 'I can't speak. I'll write it down.'

He retrieved the remains of his typewriter from the floor, put it on the desk and started clacking wildly at the keys.

Three minutes later, he'd had his say. The notette read:

'It is dangerous to talk. Russian floors have ears. Mr Big has been bugging us. Rachmaninoff told me, last time he came out of the mental institution. See that metal plate – that's it. I'm just going to defuse it and we'll be safe to talk.'

Robinski shrugged her shoulders and wondered why her non-too-intelligent boss hadn't simply taken her for a walk on Lenin Hills. But hers was not to reason why; hers was just to do and spy.

Fatman moved with quite unusual speed. After a desperate attempt to budge the huge brass screws with his fingernails, he had a flash of brilliance. He rummaged through the vast pockets of his tasteful canary yellow spy's uniform. At last he thought he'd found a screwdriver. But it was only his cock he'd grasped through a hole in one of his pockets! Not being able to bear to see him struggling so, Robinski opened her handbag and drew out just the thing he needed. It was a screwdriver – regulation issue – the small handle doubled as a container for her cyanide pills. Handing the implement to him, she had an uncharitable flash. Perhaps the death tablets would be kinder in the long run! But she put such thoughts from her mind, as she watched him beavering away at the screws. He'd got three out and started eagerly on the fourth. This one proved a little difficult. Then he had it. He beamed broadly.

The occupants of the room below did not share his mirth as three tons of crystal chandelier descended on them.

Later, it was reported in *Pravda* that most of Russia's top agents – holding their A.G.M. at the time – had been eliminated by an unidentified flying light-fitting.

So overjoyed and insensitive was our hero, that he didn't even hear the resounding crash below or feel the tremour that shook the entire building.

'Now, R-ski,' he said, using the term of endearment that illustrated his fondness for a particular part of her anatomy, 'we can talk.'

He plucked at the buttons of her blouse. They flew in all directions like popping corn. He pulled her bra roughly and her unripe melons came out for a brief breath of dismal Muscovite air. Then, popped back into their elasticated prison.

He eased her shirt down over her creamy shoulders and tugged at the sleeves. He reached behind her and expertly – for one with such fat fingers – flicked the catch of her bra. She jiggled a bit and her brassiere fell away. He buried his bullet-shaped head in her warm sweet-smelling globes. Robinski's scent was intoxicating.

Fatman caressed her soft, warm mammaries. He continued gently kneading one with his left hand, while his right hand plunged to her knickers, beneath the waistband of her skirt. The elastic sprang back obligingly. He grunted with pleasure as his fingers entered the hot and hairy world contained in her panties. The Mongolian leaned against the door; her knees began to sag. She reached out and pulled his shirt free from his trousers. Her hands fumbled momentarily with the heavy metal buckle on his belt. Seconds later, his trousers were snared around his ankles and she was burrowing into his specially-imported Marks and Spencer's best. She grabbed him expertly through the voluminous yellow drawers and began a slow, sweet milking of his stubby stalk. By now his head had sunk to her breasts. His lips fastened on to a nut-hard nipple. He looked down her body and marvelled at her curves. She had the most perfect shape he'd ever felt . . . but, then he hadn't felt many. Her skin, so soft to his touch, made the plushest velvet seem rough and loofah-like. He parted her pubic hair and fingered her eager lips. They opened at his touch. Droplets of dew drenched his digits. He straightened, raising his head until it was level with hers. Her breath was coming in noisy gulps. He could feel its warmth on his face; a torrid tropical breeze. Her eyes narrowed until they were two tiny slits of dark and gleaming lust. He moved in closer. His tongue licked along the line of her naturally-long butterfly eyelashes. Her cheeks felt like the sun-kissed peaches he'd eaten the year before on the Baltic. He inhaled deeply, breathing in the muskiness of her. His fingers were busy still between her thighs. The pliant cheeks of her arse squashed like soft fruit against the door panels. His cock hovered at the mouth of her love-tunnel. Through the coarse material of her skirt, Robinski could feel Fatman's knob nuzzling her knickers. Impatient to make contact with her flesh, Fatty twisted her skirt, and rolled it upwards. It formed a cumbersome belt around her waist. His strong arms grasped her slight form and lifted her skywards. She wrapped her legs firmly around his torso. He lowered her gingerly, until she hovered an inch above his mammoth erection. She flexed her whole body for the impact of the fuck. Her open-crotch knickers allowed him immediate entry into her dark succulent plum.* He eased her down further and further until she was utterly impaled on his cock. He began a gentle swinging motion as she clung to his broad powerful shoulders. She felt as light as a fairy, spiked on his wand! As expertly as a weightlifter, he pistoned her up and down. She felt that age-old hard knot of desire creeping from the furry mound in her crotch and suffusing her entire body in waves of passion. His cock was as snug as a 'mole' in a hole. He fired his machine gun

* *For those of you who thought I'd forgotten she still had knickers on – go back to Chapter One and start again!*

into her. As the bullets of sperm sprayed her insides, she came.

The sperm whale and his poor-puss sank to the floor in the aftermath of their knee-trembler. They lay languishing in the puddle of their love. Robinski took time to scrutinise her man's scrotum; and the rest . . . He wasn't the most attractive defector she'd ever met, but he was her guy! His head was as hairless as a coot and he had an annoying habit of sucking lollipops! His tooth was magnificent – pearly and white and extremely well cared for. The furrows in his forehead were deep enough for potato planting. His pliable bulbous nose looked as though it had been fashioned from red plasticine. In fact, at Christmas, he helped out St Nicholas by doubling for Rudolph! His body was a bit on the massive side. What could have been rolls of fat on another man, were on this one too.

But Robinski was obsessed by the sheer brute strength of this powerhouse. It contrasted sharply with her own, almost childlike, proportions. Her breasts had hardly reached maturity. They were pert and small and tilted up at the ends. Her straight, slim-hipped figure resembled a boy's. She had sinewy legs and well-toned thighs – all of her was exercised to the very peak of fitness. Especially the muscles of her fanny. She constantly practised with her faithful old government-supplied dildo; clenching and unclenching the walls of her pussy. This Cleopatra's Girdle could even take the top off a decadent, Western, coke bottle. Unfortunately, her face looked a little like the back of the fast bus from Moscow to Leningrad . . .

Coming out of their post-coital nap, Fatman decided it must be safe now to impart the extreme deviousness of his plan. He would share all with his paramour.

'Rightski, now I've had relief and we are bugless, I can spill the beans.'

Open-mouthed, Robinski hung on Fatty's every word.

'As you know, this Russian department of the Cocks

Galore Bureau (CGB), under the sinister leadership of Mr Big Balls, is pressing ahead with its intergalactic brothel chain. Spunknic Inc. has already brothelised Jupiter and Saturn and my idea, to do the same with the Earth, has really turned them on.'

Robinski stifled a yawn at this – she'd heard it all before.

'My job is to boldly seek out suitable worlds for take-over and then to mastermind the assault.'

Another yawn.

'But what my superiors don't know . . .'

Somewhere in a control room in the heart of the Gremlin building, a hand moved across a bank of switches. It stopped when it came to one marked 'Fatman'. A whirr and a click. The hand carefully twirled the knob. The tape machine started to roll, recording Fatty's every comma.

'. . . is that I have a plan of great deviousness of my own.'

Robinski sat bolt upright, her eyes wide, lips drooling and legs apart.

'What I am planning will shake the entire universe. It's all to do with . . .'

And at that moment, the joyous rattle of the tea-trolley was heard outside Fatman's inner sanctum. A loud metallic rap on the door heralded the arrival of Vladimir with elevenses. The door was kicked open by an inhuman boot and the robot/teaperson trundled in. He squeaked uncomfortably towards them and intoned:

'Tea, coffee or vodka?'

'Vodka and biscuits twice,' barked Fatman.

Vladimir spun on his shiny shins and clanked back to his trolley parked in the corridor. Vlad's mechanical arms whirred around in their sockets as he busied himself over the snacks. In a flash, the odd couple were served and Vladimir was nought but a clank in the distance.

Fatman downed the fiery liquid, while Robinski crunched thoughtfully on her digestives. He began again.

'As I was saying, I have a plan of such magnitude . . .'

The rest of his sentence was drowned by the clang of the firebell. Binski was almost trampled underfoot as Fatman fought to save himself. By the time she'd got to the door, Fatman was a wobbling blob on the horizon of the mile-long corridor. She rushed to join him outside the walls of the Gremlin. There, all the gnomes were assembled in line.

Mr Big himself was checking names on a large clip-board. He rushed around officiously from spy to spy.

'Zere are forty-eight missing,' he yelled worriedly.

A gaunt figure dressed in a grey fur hat with flaps and a matching greatcoat stepped manfully forward. His high boots crunched on the snow as he clicked his heels in deep grovel.

'There has been an accident, your Bigness. A mysterious loosening of a chandelier from its fastenings, which has eliminated nearly fifty of your top agents.'

Fatman, overhearing this little titbit, had the grace to blush. Realising his slight *faux-pas*, he shrunk into the anonymity of his yellow overalls.

This was the fourth time that week the Gremlin staff had been subjected to a fire drill. Fatman was getting pissed off with them. Now, he and Robin were both freezing; up to their knees in icy sludge. They'd be there for another hour at least while the building was thoroughly checked for incendiary devices. Fatman couldn't stand it. There'd been so many interruptions this morning already, that he decided to take Robinski and slope off to the Out-tourist Hotel for a cup of something reviving. Making sure Mr Big didn't see them leaving, they edged off towards the back of the throng. Niftily avoiding the snake-like queue of faithful peasants bent on taking a butchers at the remains of Lenin, the two interlopers plodded resourcefully away.

It was almost colder in the canteen of the hotel than it had been in Red Square. They barged their way through the tourists, who'd joined Russia's great national pastime

– *queuing in vain.* Up to the counter they pushed, grabbed a boiled egg each and stuck a chipped cup each under the hot water urn. Taking their succulent goodies, they sat in a quiet corner of the crowded room and Fatman once more started his diatribe. They were quite unaware of the lady hiding under the huge brim of a discreet sombrero. She seemed to be taking an inordinate interest in them, behind her copy of the Beanoski.

'At last we're alone,' said Fatty with a hint of irony in his voice. 'Now I can unfold my brilliant scheme for our future together. On my travels for Spunknic Inc., I've not only been working hard for the state, I've been doing a bit of research for myself.'

His eyes had a feverish glint as he continued excitedly.

'I have set in motion the first stages of my plan to start a master-race. This strain of super-beings will, of course, conquer the whole of the universe.'

'Golly gosh galactic goolies,' said Robinski, in awe at the monstrousness of her boss' idea.

'And I will lead them. I will be in complete universal control. Nothing will stop me. I will be the most powerful being in the whole history of the galaxy. I have implemented stage one of Supercede, as I've affectionately called it, and all is proceeding apace. First, I had to locate the ideal spot as a breeding ground. And in my vast interstellar trots, I happened upon the perfect place. I have just the planet up my sleeve.'

Robinski looked up his sleeve and could see nothing but his hairy armpits.

'It's well off the beaten space track. About five light years from the nearest interstellar motorway. It's not on any map – it's never been discovered. I found it. And I've named it the Planet of Eden.'

Binski gazed in rapture at her latterday Christopher Columbus.

'And the atmosphere is conducive to the super-beings

I'm going to hatch. It's dripping with luxuriant foliage. Succulent plants grow alongside tinkling brooks. All manner of exotic fruits flowers and veg. grow bountifully on the allotment I've staked. Its five suns guarantee perpetual warmth. The air is fresh and balmy, the water crystal clear, and the animal life harmless. The oceans are warm and teem with edible fish and crustacea. It's paradise. And it's all mine . . . mine . . . mine.'

In his excitement, Fatty's voice carried clear across the crowded room. The lady with the funny hat lowered her paper imperceptibly. A glint of gold flashed in her mouth, as she smiled at Fatty's unwise, bawdy indiscretions. She hadn't heard it all, but she'd heard enough . . . She would have quite a few tasty tit-bits to offer her superiors now.

Fatman waxed on, oblivious to the suspicious optics of Mr Big's agent Iva Knockabollockoff.

'I've searched for months, nay years, to find the perfect couple and I'm here to tell you that I've found the Adam and Eve like you'd never believe. The girl is a raving beauty and from good stock. She is tall, slim, lissom, long-legged, elegant, quick-witted, intellectual, far-seeing, kind, loving, sexy, and very, very fertile. She is indeed an extraordinary earthling.'

'She's willing to take part in your Supercede plan, is she?' enquired Robinski.

'She isn't aware that I've bestowed this huge honour on her person. Not as yet. She was married to a moron unfortunately. So I couldn't just kidnap them both and take them to the Planet of Eden. I've been far more subtle than that. I've found a super-alien on the planet of Spermola who is Superman to my Wonder Woman. I've been cloning in my laboratory and I've discovered the way to do it. Tom, as my superman has now to be called, has taken the exact form of this earthling's human husband. He is in situ at this very moment. He radioed me last night by intergalactic carrier pigeon. All is going according to

Supercede, the switch was effected with the minimum of fuss, and he's had intercourse without a hitch – without even arousing her suspicions. There is, of course, one gigantic snag in my masterwork.'

Robinski thought sarcastically: 'How unusual.'

Fatty's eyes narrowed as he read her silent thought.

'I know what you're thinking, you uncharitable hussy, you. But everything is going to be OK. Jim'll fix it.'

Robinski's thoughts widened as she ruminated on the fact that most things Fatty fixed had a habit of coming unstuck. He was no Superglue!

Ignoring her further disloyal wanderings, our hero, the mind-reader, plodded on:

'The snag is that although my alien can achieve orgasm and ejaculate in the humanoid way, as yet, I have not perfected the content of his come. It's completely seedless – like a satsuma. No pips at all. But I'm going to take the afternoon off work and barricade myself in my laboratory. With luck and my super intelligence, I will have sorted out my sperm problem before the ball tonight.'

CHAPTER THREE

Rock Around the Cock

Cinderella and her ugly sister arrived at the ball. Fatman and Robinski looked good in their home-made Cinders suits. Fatty was especially engaging in his ugly sister's drag. His bald pate hid under a purple shag-pile wig. It hung rakishly over his crossed eyeballs. His powder-blue gown billowed wildly from the neck; for all the universe giving him the appearance of a pregnant duck! He teetered dangerously on his fourteen-inch platforms.

Robinski looked charming in her simple rags. Her one perverted extravagence, was a pair of shoes with flat mirror buckles. She was knickerless and her pudenda shone brightly from her feet. Her footwear had been a gift from Fatman; and yet another example of his peculiar sexual tastes.

Fatman was not in high good humour. His semen tests had been an utter failure. He'd been battling with test tubes of sperm all afternoon. To no avail. Still, tonight he would put it out of his mind and try to enjoy this top agents' ball. Everyone, but everyone, in the secret service was there. From the lowliest phone-tapper to Mr Big Balls himself. The latter had outdone all the other costumed revellers by covering himself in loose skin and saying he'd come as a scrotum.

A tall dark stranger dressed as a daffodil waltzed past Fatman and Robinski, clutching a lady with a sombrero. As this bizarre duo paso-dobled on, the mysterious sombreroed woman caught Fatman's eye. For some extraordinary reason she flashed him a smile and he caught a glint of gold between her ruby lips.

'A very rich Russian woman to be able to afford such a tooth,' he thought.

Meanwhile, scrotum-features leant against the bar. Fatman watched him like a hawk; always on the alert for an indiscretion amongst the senior ranks, with which he might blackmail his way even higher up the spy-ral.

Wilhelm and the Vomits came to the end of a particularly feverish numero and went straight into an even-more up-tempo tune.

Iva Knockabollockoff dispatched the daffodil and decided to sit this one out, keeping her eye on Fatperson all the while. She chose a table close to his, from which she'd have a fine view of her corpulent prey. Nonchalantly, she tipped back her hat until it fell over her shoulders.

A shadow fell across her face. She looked up and saw only the huge outline of the man, who had an arm outstretched in invitation. He threaded his way through the gyrating dancers pulling her behind him. The beat was forcing the dancers into the most elaborate contortions. But this man didn't heed the pulsating rhythm. She could smell his Paco Rabanne, even before she melted into his arms. He encircled her waist with an arm and pulled her to him. She caught her breath as her breasts were viciously crushed against his ribcage of steel. She tried to push away but his arms were like metal bands encasing her taut body. She relaxed. He didn't. She began to feel an insistent hard lump in her groin. It bit into the pliant flesh of her thigh.

She tilted her head back and looked up into the smouldering eyes. They were two dark pools of lust. Lights flashed suddenly and illuminated the stranger's face. He was a stranger no longer. The eyes that bore into her belonged to Mr Big. Shock, horror and delight coursed through her very being. He saw her register recognition and a smile twitched at the corners of his mobile mouth.

'I'm going to screw you on the dancefloor,' he said conversationally.

'Nice,' she thought, not knowing whether to come or faint. She did neither. Instead, she juiced the narrow bridge of her skimpy briefs.

All around the ardent couple, people flung themselves energetically in all directions. Abruptly, the beat changed and the Vomits broke into a traditional slow Russian smooch. Some dancers were arrested in mid-twirl; others halted in mid-hustle. The lights were dimmed even further. Crotches ground into crotches. Arms twined around overheated torsos.

Noticing something was up on the dance floor, Fatso got to his feet and took his Cinderella to the ball, or balls to be precise – Mr Big Balls. The boss, thinking he was safely hemmed in on all sides, started his assault on the busty body beside him. Deftly, he caught hold of the hem of her skirt and pulled it skywards. She sensed, rather than heard, a zip descend.

By this time, Fatman had arrived one couple away, with his spy's survival kit at the ready. Hidden in the palm of his hand was the tiny lighter that doubled as a miniature camera. He began clicking at the same time as Iva felt the urgency of a fleshy knob pressing into her knickers.

The smoochy music crooned on as Mr Big continued his sexual manoeuvres. A hand wormed its way down the front of her dress and fondled her left breast. A thumbscrew began; her nipple was the target. The acorn-sized bud was roughly tweaked, then twisted around and around. It brought tears to her eyes and warmth to her crotch. She looked wildly in all directions – surely someone must have noticed his actions. All the dancers appeared to be wrapped up in each other, however, and she certainly didn't notice Fatman's infra-red camera clicking away discreetly but merrily close by. It was obvious that Mr Big didn't notice either. He followed her glances, then shook his head from side to side.

'We're safe!' he whispered.

His teeth bared in a smile, his mouth found hers and his tongue pushed its way rudely between her lips. Down, down, down her throat, the pink moist intruder went. Meanwhile, below, another longer, pinker intruder was seeking entry. With a sharp yank, he moved the crotch of her knickers to one side. The elastic twanged painfully against her leg, as he aimed his cock in the direction of her opening. For a second, it flayed around in the warm hairy cellar of her drawers. Then, it speared her. Her insides became liquidescent at the touch of his cock. Their feet stopped moving to the music as their organs ground to the stronger beat of their desire. He lunged forward again and again but only the tip was allowed into her hole. Shuddering at the warmth, the smell, the closeness of Mr Big, Iva stiffened suddenly. And so did Balls. The excitement of his entry in so public a place was too much for her and almost too much for Fatman's camera. She lost control and started her ascension to pleasure. The bubble of intense desire forming within her, began to burst; pricked into action. Her head fell forwards on to his manly chest. She *had* to come. Nothing could stop the rush of lust to her loins. If a spotlight had splashed over them, she could not have stopped. She bit her bottom lip to stop herself screaming out loud in ecstacy. And so did Fatman. She came. Her body shook as though she was sobbing and racked with pain. The wave of sexual pleasure washed over her, leaving her once more aware of her surroundings. Embarrassed, she pulled away and her knickers twanged back into shape. The pink full-bodied penis was shut out of the life-giving well. She felt its throbbing fullness against her stomach. Mr Big growled angrily. He hadn't had his pleasure. And my Lord would have his pleasure!

'Wank me. Send me into orbit,' he commanded.

Gingerly, her hand circled the big pole which had come between them, or rather hadn't! Once more, she looked around furtively. Fatman was clumsily fitting his zoom lens for a closer look at Mr Big's equipment, but again she didn't see him.

'Wank me,' came the insistent order.

Surreptitiously, she started strumming his stalk. It bounced like rubber in her palm; a slippery, slurping, sex-starved eel. The first tell-tale warnings of impending orgasm squeezed out of the tiny eye in its red and swollen head. She pressed into him, trying to shield his exposed self with her body. Frustrated by this movement, Fatman two-stepped nearer. Mr Balls began to pant. Short, peculiar gasps broke from his lips. He was well on the boil. And what was she supposed to do with the liquid that was about to spurt in all directions? Surely, the dancers would notice a shower of this big man's ball-syrup. She clutched the randy robot even harder. He screamed and came. Frantically, she cupped a hand over the top of the fountain to stop the never-ending stream of milky white jissome. She longed to lick him clean but just had to make do. She rubbed the sticky propogative substance into the taut satin skin of his stick. She continued to massage the length of his rod, being careful not to touch the tender, sensitive spot that was the centre of his sex. His breathing slowed. Soon there was hardly a trace of cream. The cat licked her lips. She withdrew her honeyed hand and adjusted her clothes. Her skirt fell back into place. Masses of guilty creases were visible down the front of the garment. He slipped his cock neatly back into his jock cage.

Fatman was off the dance floor within seconds, dragging the long-suffering Robinski behind him. They dashed for an emergency exit and rushed past the security guards. Three and a half minutes later, they were safely ensconsced in the agent's darkroom. The two huddled over his tanks. Fatman's fingers fumbled with the latch of the miniature camera.

'I've got him Robin,' cried Fatman. 'This is extra insurance for a meteoric rise in my career. I can blackmail him. He will have to help us in our bid for total power, otherwise I will expose him.'

'Who was she? I couldn't make her out in the dark,' hissed Robinski clinging to her lover's ample biceps, and shaking with excitement. There was a click and the camera back sprang open.

'This is it,' yelped Fatman, as he thrust in two stubby fingers to grip the end of the film. He pulled violently on nothing and ended up on the floor. His ruddy face turned ashen as he realised what had happened.

'There was no film in the camera,' he cried.

CHAPTER FOUR

MaCabre Knees

The house on Loch McCock shuddered as the roof caved in. Violet, peeling potatoes at the time, screamed as large pieces of plaster showered around her.

'Another of those bloody missiles from the space station's gone awry,' she thought uncharitably.

But poor Violet was wrong. This was a direct hit! As more plasterwork descended into her bowl of peelings, Violet got the feeling that she ought to investigate the earthquake. Wiping her hands on her pinny, she shuffled through to the living room. As she entered the salon, a piece of white masonry dive-bombed on her head. The poor woman saw stars and then blackness engulfed her.

Minutes before Violet's untimely accident, Peggy Sue had been flying through the air with the greatest of ease; daring young bint that she was. She wheeled through the atmosphere, enjoying the feel of the crisp Scots air through her paper-thin apparel. She played with her steering toggles, turning herself this way and that as her slow descent continued. For her final approach to the landing pad in the garden, Peggy turned on her strings and headed for home.

'Shiiiit!' she screamed as one of the toggles came off in her hand.

Desperation gripped her. She attempted to scrabble for the cords of her chute. But to no avail. She was without steering or direction! Totally at the mercy of her chute. She shot forwards and realised she was going to miss her landing patch and it looked as if she'd wrap herself around the chimney of McCock House. Lower and lower she went, with the roof of the building whizzing towards her. She shut her eyes waiting for the impact, closely followed by death. The gods were with her, however. She narrowly missed the smoke-stack and hit a weak spot in the flat roof of the lounge extension. Her last recollection was being up to the neck in plaster and then her brain blacked out. Unconscious, she slithered on through the roof and down through the ceiling of the lounge. The cords of her chute snagged on the central joist and she swung there suspended. And this was the precise second when Violet joined her in the land of Nod.

Violet lay motionless on the floor. And Peggy hung motionless from the ceiling. Tom burst through the door.

'Had a wonderful time darling,' he screamed in the direction of the hanging Peglet. 'I won first prize. Must say that this outfit you sorted out for me really went down a bomb.'

Tom was wearing a charming little two-piece in tweed. The skirt came to just below his knees. His shapely legs were encased in thick lisle stockings. On his feet were a pair of Quiet-Puppy brogues. His wig was of the silkiest texture; grey-rinsed. On his nose, he wore a pair of diamante, winged spectacles.

'They loved my Mary Whitehouse,' added Tom, as he adjusted the two huge balloons under his cashmere.

Completely ignoring Peggy's predicament, Tom bumbled on: 'Would you like a little nightcap darling? I know it's after five in the morning but let's have a little something before you turn in. Then I must away to my shed.'

He crossed to the drinks' cabinet and poured out two large ones. Retracing his steps with a glass in each hand, Tom stopped underneath his swinging wife. He looked up. Realisation dawned.

'Oh, another new position. I'll need the Kama Sutra and a step-ladder for this one. Won't be a tick . . . '

Tom rushed out of the room, striding over Violet on his way. Just then a face appeared at the window. Two quizzical violet eyes surveyed the shattered scene. They disappeared in the direction of the front door. It creaked open and a shaft of sunlight spilled into the gloomy room. Two unmistakable knees beneath an unmistakable kilt tiptoed into the room – in an unmistakable fashion!

Realising Peggy's precarious position, the stranger bounded across the room and stood under the hanging girl. Looking up at her, he noticed that she was beginning to revive.

Peggy's eyes flickered open and she surveyed him with incredulity. A question formed at the back of her throat . . .

'I've come about the Martians,' he said.

The shock was too much for the poor girl and she moved on her moorings, moaning softly.

'Martians,' he reiterated.

The plaster groaned as Peggy tried to wriggle free. An eerie creak heralded her descent. The stranger looked up, only to see the split-moon of Peg's crotch crashing down towards him. As she landed full on top of him and slid down his face, he caught a whiff of her sweet perfume. Then he joined Violet . . . out like a light.

The scrape of wood on wood was heard as Tom dragged a large pair of wooden steps through the doorway. He positioned them carefully under the spot where his wife had recently been hanging. Lifting his skirts, he mounted the wobbly staircase. He got to the summit and found the parachute harness was bare. Completely mystified, his eyes wandered heavenward to see if Peggy had retraced her steps and gone out the way she'd come in. A voice came from the four-legged octopus on the floor. Peggy poked her head from the mess of limbs.

'What the fuck are you doing up there?' she asked her husband in exasperation. 'I'm down here on top of this man. I think I've killed him.'

'Who did you say he is?' asked the befuddled Tom from his make-shift vantage point. 'Oh, never mind, sod him. I thought you wanted to swing from the chandelier.'

'You have a one-track dirt-track mind. Can you think of nothing else when there's two people down here needing first aid? Do you think he's dead? And what about poor Violet over there?'

'I'm sure he'll be OK,' countered Tom, crest-fallen on his ladder. 'And as for Violet – look, the plaster's twitching even as I speak.'

Violet raised herself from her bed of bricks and mortar and hobbled into the kitchen, thinking that a cup of tea might be appropriate in the circumstances.

Undeterred by the somnambulent stranger's presence, Tom raised his skirt and sashayed down the ladder.

'Look it won't hurt if we have a quick one,' he said nonchalantly to Peggy, his cock waving in the air.

Peggy passed over the penis.

'I'm going to check his pulse,' she said.

She reached down between the legs of the stranger. And simultaneously surveyed her Timex.

'He's OK,' she said, after half a minute. 'Don't just stand there waving it,' she continued, pointing at Tom's cock, 'do something useful!'

As Tom aimed at Peggy's crotch, the stranger on the floor sat up and received a sharp poke in the eye with Tom's very blunt instrument.

'I suppose it's better than being poked in the eye with a

sharp stick,' he quipped, rubbing his damaged optic.

He reared up between husband and wife. He had a large egg-shaped lump on the side of his head, where Peggy had hit a bullseye with her pudenda. Tom's erection withered at the sight of the reviving interloper. He dropped his skirt, deftly concealing his chopper in the length of tweed.

'What are you doing here?' said the master of the house. 'Who are you?'

The piss-taking stranger looked at Tom: 'Who is this lady?'

'That's no lady, that's my husband,' said the unabashed Peggy.

'Oh, he's one of them . . . ' answered the intruder.

'Oh, no he's not,' Peggy said.

'Oh, yes he is.'

'Tom, he's delerious, help me restrain him.'

'I'm on the job,' said the stranger. 'Looking for escaped Martians. I've just seen two in your garden and I thought you were another one of those.'

'Don't start that again!' Peggy eyed him with exasperation.

'Well, they look just like you . . . '

'How dare you sir. My wife looks nothing like a Martian.' Tom reared to the defence of Peggy.

'What's she wearing then?' the new arrival asked.

'Just a little something I threw on . . . '

'Looks like you very nearly missed! Martians . . . they're clever little buggers. They can change their shape at will. And their favourite form is that of a naked female human. I've been put on the job because I can resist their deadly charms.'

'Oh really,' said Peggy getting into the swing of the joking. 'Tom, *he* is one of them . . . '

'I'm not standing here a single second longer listening to this bilge,' said Tom. 'Furthermore, I don't wish to discuss my wife's nationality with the likes of you. Be off with you.'

The stranger, realising his time was running out, like sand through an hour glass, made to go. He raised his body up on his elbows and manfully tried to get to his feet. Each time he attempted to put weight on his left foot, it gave way and he winced loudly with the pain. Peggy felt a wave of sympathy for the man whose face she'd sat so heavily upon. By now, the mysterious person was flat on his back again, wracked with pain.

'I know,' said Peggy, 'I'll give him the kiss of life – that'll do the trick.'

The stranger puckered up obligingly, when Tom interfered.

Gnashing his teeth like a blood-starved vampire, Tom bore down on the recumbent invalid.

This seemed to revive the cripple somewhat: 'Where's the garlic?' he screeched, making the sign of the cross with his hand as Tom moved even closer. 'I don't kiss men with lipstick,' he added unnecessarily.

Tom, in a slow, evil manner, drew the back of his hand across his mouth and removed all traces of the paint.

'So, you do kiss men without,' he continued eagerly in an unprecedented homosexual outburst.

Peggy looked preoccupied. She glanced at her watch. 'It's nearly six Tom, you've only a few minutes left . . . '

'What, before he self-destructs?' interjected the joker in the pack.

'Blast,' oathed Tom, 'and I'd been hoping we'd have time for a fuck before I have to shut myself away in my intergalactic lean-to.'

'I suppose he has to be shut away before anyone else notices the balloons up his jumper and mascara dripping off his fangs.'

'Don't be so rude,' Peggy told their unwanted guest.

Marching over to the inert invalid, Tom, obviously

losing patience, barked: 'Come on you, I've had enough of your lip. I want you to shove off before I shack up in the shed.'

Reaching down, he grabbed the man by the shoulder. With an enormous heave, Tom got him to his feet, only to have the unfortunate pass out with the pain.

'He's left the land of the living again,' Peggy said concerned.

'He wasn't alive was he?' retorted Tom, 'I thought I even saw a touch of *rigor mortis* between the legs!'

'I'm not sure Tom. I still think we ought to look at him more closely. I'll strip him from this end,' Peggy pointed at the weird man's head, 'and expose his private parts.'

'And who's going to handle my privates?' said the stranger, rearing up.

'I was going to put my gardening gloves and wellies on for that,' Tom spat out.

The stranger realised that Tom's patience was wearing ice-thin. Once more, he attempted lift-off from the floor. But he couldn't make it – his ankle was too painful. Peggy took control. She marched over to the intruder, seized him by the collar and dragged him agonisingly to the sofa. En route, she felt a hand creep around and caress the soft underside of her left breast. 'Cheeky devil,' she thought, throwing the gate-crasher face-down into the bosom of leather. He sank into the hide chaise-longue with a noisy fart, and squirmed around until he was lying full-stretch on the settee.

Peggy thought it was time for introductions:

'My name is Peggy and this is my husband Tom. He's an arse – '

'Oh really?' interrupted the squatter.

' – tronaut,' she went on, paying no heed. 'I'm so sorry to have dropped in on you like that. I hope I haven't broken any of your credentials.'

'That's all right,' said the stranger, 'I just love people sitting on my face.'

'For goodness sake, stop worrying about him,' said Tom, 'I shouldn't think any part of him is essential. He shouldn't have been snooping around here in the first place, anyway.'

The stranger, whether from his injuries or from Tom's insults, flushed bright red.

'I say Peggy, I don't like the way he's puffing up,' said Tom with a new hint of concern in his voice. 'And I don't like his colour much either.'

'Don't be rude, Tom, it may be his own. Goodness knows what he looked like before I fell on him.'

'I wonder if he has damaged anything, though?' said Tom feeling up the cuckoo's kilt.

'Don't touch what you can't afford,' said the interloper.

Peggy moved in on the sofa. The leather squeaked as she knelt astride the stranger's torso.

'How does this feel?' she asked.

Her hands massaged his shoulders and across his chest. Her long blonde hair trailed lightly across his face. Her fingers explored on and down his manly body. Something stirred beneath the tartan. She slipped a hand under the rough material of the Scotsman's shirt. Her agitated husband leapt from foot to foot as the Scotsman's monster rose towards the seat of her passion. Noticing the haggis-hopping going on under the man's sporran, Peggy quickly removed her hand from his shirt. Her abrupt action caused the jock to jerk in his seat and his kilt rucked up. Peggy shrieked as she caught a quick flash of his knees.

Luckily Violet chose that moment to enter with a trolley, laden with hot griddle scones and a pot of scalding tea. Peggy, under cover of this distraction, fled to her husband's side and whispered to him.

'Those MaCabre knees. It's him. The one with the binoculars. The one that's been watching me all the time you've been away. I'd remember those knees. I'd recognise them anywhere. They're more dimpled than Kirk Douglas' chin.'

Tom, not one for beating about the bush, strode across the room and enquired of the stranger: 'Here, who are you? And why've you been watching my wife?'

'I am with the Intergalactic CIB.'

'You mean CID,' corrected Tom.

'No, CIB. Casual Indiscriminate Banging.'

Tom, beginning to look decidedly ill-at-ease, said softly: 'You mean you're a space policeman.'

'Yes. My name's Navek. And I'm the officer in charge of the Martian-hunting department.'

Tom's face continued to fall at these words. The blood seemed to be draining from his body. Peggy felt, though she knew it must surely be her imagination, that her husband was getting smaller. His whole person seemed to be shrivelling away.

The clock struck six. And Tom, ashen faced, fled from the room.

'Whatever's wrong with him?' queried Navek.

'Oh, he's got some important experiments that he's doing for his space station. They need attention every six hours. He'll be locked away in his lab for at least an hour. I've strict instructions never to disturb him. The experiments are delicate and can, all too easily, be ruined if the timing isn't exact.'

Navek raised an eyebrow.

'I'm glad he's gone. I've got something of the utmost importance to tell you. As you realise, I've been watching you for the past few weeks. I'm using the Martian hunt as a cover. It's my usual line of work. But the reason I'm here in Scotland, dragged up in a kilt, all concerns a message which someone in my department intercepted. It was on its way to Moscow. Now, we've decoded as much of it as we can and your name keeps cropping up. But we still don't know what the connection is. The message has definitely been sent from this island. Have you any idea what all this is about?'

Peggy sat down shaking her head. 'I've no idea what you're talking about. Are you sure this message mentioned me? And why can't you decode it all?'

Navek looked embarrassed. He couldn't tell her the whole story. He'd have to think of an excuse.

He remembered so well the day his secretary had come rushing into his office, with a smile on her face and come in her knickers. She had been so excited at intercepting a top-priority broadcast to the Russians that she could hardly contain her excitement or her love juice! She'd run breathlessly up to him, her breasts bouncing and bobbing delightfully in the confines of her woolly. He could still see the outline of her massive thighs as she'd strode to his side. The material had ridden up between her legs and had moulded to the shape of her mons. He'd seen the first signs of wetness which had quickly spread from her knickers into the weave of her skirt. Her round cheeks had been flushed a healthy shade of pink.

Her full lips had parted prettily as she'd looked up at him. He'd felt the hard nuggets of her nipples drilling into his chest. She'd waved the piece of paper in her hand. Dazed by the sheer size and vitality of her, Navek knew he'd have to have her there and then. He'd known he had to sink between her fleshy thighs and had to dunk his wick in her deep pool of passion.

'Never mind the message,' he'd said. 'Lock the door.'

She'd turned and run quickly to the door. He'd followed her amazing dancing buttocks and had known, then, they were bare. The twin cheeks of her rear end had moved like mountainous jellies before him. He'd stiffened in his serge. She'd borne down on him. His eyes had tried to focus on her mobile mammaries. Once more, Ophelia's odour had surrounded him. A cloud of lust had dimmed his very senses. The paper in her hand had fluttered to the floor.

She'd followed, as Navek had spreadeagled her on the broadloom. He'd mounted her body and lain with his hard knot pressing into the soft billowing flesh of her hot belly. His head had disappeared in the angora-smothered chest. Navek's hand had slipped under the bunny fluff and had tried to grasp one mammary peak. His hand, at full stretch, hadn't been able to encompass the doughy mound. Two hands had managed to cover one breast but still there'd been overspill. His cock had been so hot and hard that it had almost speared its way through his trousers.

Ophelia had smiled; had known his predicament well. A large pudgy hand had tugged at his zip and ripped open his fly, manhandling his member with great aplomb. He had moved to accommodate the luscious large lady. Navek had squeezed the big breast into a point and had placed the inch of nipple stalk between his lips. It had been like sucking a miniature cock. The nipple had grown in dimension as his tongue had circumnavigated its huge head. The awesome thing had made to choke him. He had felt it hard against the back of his throat.

'What beautiful tits,' he'd thought, as he'd chewed on into wonderland.

His cheeks had bulged, as the nipple duelled with his tongue. Meanwhile, his knob had been pummelled by a bunch of live bananas. A thumb, almost as big as his cock, had steadied the flaying randy rod. His stalk had been strummed with a strong right hand. He'd wanted to cry out for a lighter touch but at the same time beg for rougher, tougher treatment. She'd tugged his tool as he'd fed upon a feast tit for a king!

Pain had shot through his body. She had lifted him by his cock. The rubbery folds had slid from his grasp. He'd sped upwards, sure she'd tried to tear his trunk from its roots. All she'd wanted, though, had been to have his seed stalk between her oversized melons. She'd squashed them in, until his cock had been trapped by tons of tit. The pain had receded and pleasure had taken its place. He'd wallowed in the titty tunnel, as happy as a hippo in mud. Her strong legs had twined around his. He'd placed his hands on the floor, at either side of her magnificent body. So positioned, he had steadied himself. He'd pressed up and down, had slid his bolt into a lock of breasts. It had been a tiny worm crawling between two giant mobile molehills. All at once, she'd taken hold of his head and shoved, pushing it away, way down her body and between her thighs. His lips had come to rest half an inch above hers and his eyes had beheld her hairy honeypot. Its red eye had winked at him and its lips puckered in a kiss of lust. The next thing he'd known was that his head had been imprisoned in a mantrap of flesh. Walls of soft womanhood had crushed in on his head. He'd been sucked into paradise. He'd floated on an ocean of juicy joy-liquid. His tongue had dived into her muff and he'd tasted her pink cavern. Her legs had locked around his head and he'd been almost strangled in her love-vice. He'd felt her urgent passion rising to fever pitch. She'd screamed. She'd sighed. And she'd let his head roll free from the tight trap of her thighs. He'd started his long trek up her mountainous slopes and had pushed his pinkie between her perkies yet again. She'd scooped her breasts together and had pushed inwards; had trapped his raging rod between her creamy orbs. The velvet touch of her ample boobs had sent his sperm rocketing up his shaft. It had hesitated in the head for the briefest of seconds and had then flown in all directions. Later, when they'd recovered their composure and rearranged their clothes, they'd discovered to their horror, that portions of the decoded message had been completely obliterated by large dollops of come. In vain, they'd tried to wipe off the sticky substance but it had clung like glue to the page.

Coming out of his Ophelia-inspired reverie, he heard Peggy enquire: 'Look, I've asked you three times, you seem to be in a daze. Why haven't you decoded all of the message?'

Red-faced, Navek replied: 'I know this sounds really stupid, but my secretary spilt tea over it. And all that was left was your name and address and something about a super-race. At first, I thought you were involved, but having watched you incessantly these last few weeks, you don't seem to do anything suspicious except fuck a lot.'

'So, it was you who was watching us in the heather,' Peggy spat. 'We *were* being watched. I told Tom but he wouldn't believe me.'

'Look, if it's not you, somebody here – and that only leaves your housekeeper Violet and your husband Tom – is communicating with the other side. I know Violet's OK . . .'

Outside the door, Tom's ear was pressed firmly to the keyhole. Little did Navek know that he was sealing his own and Violet's fate with these few ill-chosen words. Tom hadn't gone to his shed – he'd been listening all the while . . .

' . . . she's one of our agents. Have you noticed anything strange about your husband recently? Has he been acting oddly in any way? Is he different?'

Peggy brushed him off: 'Don't be so silly. He's only just arrived back from his space station.'

'Think back over the time he's been here this time. Hasn't anything aroused your suspicions?'

Peggy looked blank. Then, the trace of a frown creased her brow.

'He did have an uncharacteristic burst of violence just after he arrived, when I introduced him to Ms Tree – Violet. He slapped her around the face . . . twice. And, when he flew in, he was silent for ages. He didn't speak at all.'

'What *did* he do then?' Navek enquired.

Peggy turned from him, blushing: 'It's slightly embarrassing. He walked out of his spaceship and just took me on the heather. He didn't even say "hello". And I had the most peculiar feeling – when he was making love to me. One of his hands was pulling away at my flying suit, while another toyed with a nipple. And, I know it sounds impossible, but I was sure I felt a third hand between my legs. I opened my eyes and looked down but I'm certain there were only two hands at work.'

Navek's face turned to stone. Tom moved from the door and scurried off to his garden laboratory. Somewhere along the path from the house to the shed, which was built against the garden wall, Tom disappeared. The creature that let himself into the lab with Tom's one and only key was green, jelly-like and only three foot high. It appeared to have no definite appendages but could take any shape at will. As it stood at the door to the shed, an arm appeared from the jelly casing and turned the key. Once inside, the alien wobbled over to a workbench and started mixing potions from Baby Bio bottles. Its two strange hands worked at a feverish pace with the liquid. It filled a syringe with the thick red goo and jabbed the needle into its green matter. Seconds later, Tom was standing there, fussing over his bench.

CHAPTER FIVE

Things that go green in the night . . . or the day

Tom sat at his workbench waiting for his message. The radio set crackled and Fatman's voice burst through the static.

'Major Tom,' said the loudspeaker. 'Are you receiving me? Over.'

'Major Tom to ground control. I am receiving you, over.'

'I've been working all day with these bloody test tubes, Tom, and I still haven't cracked the secret of the sperm. But I'm persevering and Robinski's helping. There is one problem, however, I'm running out of semen and you might have to send me some more. A few tubesful express post would help.'

Fatman continued: 'Is everything all right there. Does Peggy suspect anything? How are you adjusting to human life? Over.'

'She doesn't know,' replied Tom. 'But this fellow called Navek has just barged in.'

'Describe him,' barked Fatman, his blood running cold.

'He's male, Caucasian, dark-haired, weighs about 200 pounds, five eleven tall and has a big cock. He says he's here investigating runaway Martians. He says they've escaped from the retention centre in the space station over on the mainland.'

'Have you left him alone with Peggy?' asked the boss in Moscow.

'I had to,' said Tom, 'it was time for another injection. I was beginning to turn green. But I did listen to his inquisition of Peggy as long as was alienly possible. Navek has sowed the seeds of doubt in her mind. He's jogged her memory and she's recalled a couple of strange incidents, when I acted out of her husband's character. It was during my adjustment phase, when I found it difficult to take on all the nuances of Tom's character.'

As Fatman turned anger-red in his Muscovite hideaway, Peggy, listening at the door of the lean-to, turned fright-white.

She had crept out there to tell Tom what Navek had been saying about him. After all, he was her husband and she did love him and, although he'd been a little strange of late, she didn't really believe the things that the intruder had told her. How could she possibly trust a man whose face she'd sat on briefly and who had let a most important message get covered in tea? She'd had her hand on the doorknob, when she'd heard Tom's voice mention Navek. And the conversation that followed sent a shiver to her brain. Who was Tom talking to in his garden shed? She sank to her knees and applied her eye to the keyhole. What she saw did nothing to allay her fears. She could just see Tom sitting amidst bottles and jam jars. He was in front of a large radio set bristling with knobs. He spoke into a shiny new microphone and replies boomed out of nowhere.

'You'll have to eliminate him,' said the invisible man.

'Well, that shouldn't be too difficult,' replied Tom. 'He's sprained his ankle and can't move for the moment. It'll be the simplest thing to carry him to my amphibious car and drown him on the way across the loch.'

Peggy's hand flew to her mouth to stifle a cry of anguish.

'My only problem will be to uproot the seeds of suspicion from Peggy's mind. And I'll have to dispose of the maid too. She's on Navek's payroll. I need some more serum. Arrange a drop for this afternoon.'

'Make sure nothing else goes wrong,' commanded Fatman. 'Over and out.'

Tom sat there, tapping his fingers thoughtfully, while he pondered his next move. Outside, a weak-kneed Peggy leaned against the wooden shack for support – near hysterical – as jumbled images flashed through her mind. If Tom wasn't Tom, where was Tom? What had these evil plotters done with him? And when had the switchover taken place? She had made love to this inhuman replica! Her clit curled up at the edges at the thought.

Movements within the shed brought her back to sanity. She dashed back into the house. Navek saw her as she flung herself through the front door. She stumbled into the room, blanched with fright. Her words poured out in an unintelligible jumble:

'Green . . . radio . . . sperm . . . Tom!'

'Get a hold on yourself,' soothed Navek. 'Slow down and tell me what's been happening.'

White-faced and shaking, Peggy crossed the room to the drinks table, poured herself and Navek two very large brandies and handed him one. She gulped greedily at the calming liquid. Pacing up and down she quickly explained what she'd heard through the lean-to door. She was scared stiff that, at any moment, Tom or whoever it was, might walk in and interrupt her before she could finish telling Navek her story. Pulling her down on the sofa beside him, Navek rested a hand on her thigh in an effort to calm her.

'It's all right. I know what's going on now. It's all beginning to fit together. I've got an agent in Moscow. She's wormed her way into becoming Mr Big's most trusted top agent. Mr Big, by the way, is the head of the CGB. She's informed me that he's instructed her to tail a couple called

Fatman and Robinski – that's who Tom's lookalike was talking to just now. From the pieces of information Iva Knockabollockoff has fed me and the extra gen you overheard, I'm pretty sure I've got the whole story now.

'Fatman is out to rule the universe. And he's chosen you for the role of Planet-Mother. He's obviously replaced your husband with an alien super-stud. But he can only keep human shape six hours at a time. This is why Tom keeps going off to his shed. He's not doing an experiment, as he told you, but goes there to inject himself with a serum and to radio Fatman.'

'What are we going to do?' wailed Peggy. 'And will I ever see my real husband again?'

'I can't answer that I'm afraid. He may still be alive. But you're going to have to be very strong. You're in no danger as long as Tom and Fatman remain ignorant of your acquaintance with their plan. When Tom comes back, you'll have to act as if nothing's happened; as if you know nothing. I know it will be difficult but, after all, he does *look* like the man you married. As for me and Violet, we're in mortal danger! And you're going to have to help us. He won't do anything while you're here; so just make sure that until my ankle gets better you don't leave him alone with me. Now, go and get Violet and I'll alert her . . . '

'There's one thing you've forgotten,' said Peggy worriedly. 'Unless I tell Tom you were asking questions about him, he'll think it really suspicious. After all, he heard every word we said when he was listening outside the door.'

'Are you up to it?' enquired Navek.

'I'll have to be,' said our heroine.

Taking her courage in both hands, Peggy marched off to confront the ogre-in-husband's-clothing.

While she was so engaged, Navek quickly filled in Violet about what had been going on. He told her that she'd have to watch Tom. She'd have to follow him when he went to pick up his serum from the appointed place of the drop.

He had no idea whether it was on the island or the mainland. She'd just have to follow him wherever he went. He impressed upon her the danger she was in. If she was seen by Tom in pursuit, it would be the end of her.

Violet understood – she had been in similar scrapes before. She scurried back into the kitchen, explaining that she'd make some breakfast – an unsuspicious thing to do and it was about that time anyway.

Soon after, she called Tom and Peggy in to get it. Navek was pleased to see that Tom's reaction to his supposed wife seemed near-to-normal – as far as he could judge. So, the alien had been outwitted by the attractive young girl. The morning passed slowly, with the three habitués of McCock House battling against a pregnant pause here and an embarrassed silence there. Right on cue, at twelve noon, Tom made his 'experiment' excuses and left Peggy and Navek to their own devices. The strain was visibly showing on Peggy's face. Her mask slipped as Tom left the room.

'Come over here,' Navek whispered.

Peggy crossed the room and sat on the edge of the sofa beside him.

'You're doing so well,' he commended. 'And I think you'll make it through whatever horrors we yet have to face. Look, as soon as that thing in the shed has had its jab, it'll be going off to pick up more serum. Violet's going to follow. So, everything's going according to plan. Don't worry . . .'

He gently placed a hand on her shoulder and gave a reassuring squeeze. Peggy turned and flung her arms around Navek's shoulders.

'I don't know whether I can keep it up,' she sobbed.

'Oh, you'll be fine,' said her strong protector, his arms purposefully encircling her waist.

Peggy's head was buried into Navek's shoulder. Small splutters of fear still escaped her lips.

'Quiet now,' he soothed and brushed a kiss on to her cheek.

Peggy responded, easing around to face him. The two moved slowly together; their lips met and Navek's tongue snaked its way into Peggy's mouth. The long kiss seemed to force new confidence into the worried girl.

'But what if Tom comes back?' whispered Peggy.

'It'll be all right,' comforted Navek, as he moved a hand down to Peggy's waist and began to feel his way inside her tight, figure-hugging flying suit.

Just then, Ms Tree came dashing into the room.

'Tom's going off!' she screamed.

'I thought he *was* off,' joked Navek, trying to make light of the sombre situation.

'I'll take the other canoe and go after him . . . ' spat Violet as she sped out of the door.

'What are we going to do now?' sobbed Peggy.

'There's only one thing to do,' returned Navek, looking her straight in her crotch, '. . . wait.'

'OK.'

'Why don't you go upstairs for a rest, Peg?' said Navek, pushing the previous moment of passion from his mind.

'All this has certainly given me a bit of a headache and I didn't get to bed at all last night . . . '

With that Peggy took herself upstairs.

She came out of her forty winks to find Navek lying on her. His head lay heavily on her breast. His leg was curled across her body. She was squashed to the bed.

'Tom!'

'No it's me . . . Navek,' he whispered in her ear.

'What's got into you?' queried the befuddled girl.

'I thought we could find solace in each other's arms . . . ' came the reply.

'But what about Tom,' said the wooden Peg, on tenderhooks.

'Violet radioed in a few moments ago. A thick mist has

come down on the mainland and Tom's gone off to the pub. She thinks it'll be a couple of hours before they're able to make the drop. So, we've got plenty of time . . .'

Doubts flashed through Peggy's mind. Was it fair to Tom, her real husband, to allow herself to be taken by this virtual stranger? But, oh, how she needed human cock comfort at this moment.

Throwing caution to the wind, she moved her arms down to crush his head into her softness and ground her pelvis against his taut torso. He slid down her body. She opened her thighs and tucked her right leg under her. His face came to rest in the hollow of her left thigh; his lips six inches from her sex. She moved his knees apart so she could see his fine fucking machinery. Her hand snaked down and started an experienced touch-up of his balls. She looked down at him. He made love with his eyes and his voice.

'You're so beautiful, Peggy. You're such a beautiful woman. I just want to enjoy you . . .'

He was in no hurry to sink deep within her. He *knew* he would have her. And he knew, she knew, that he knew. His hand caressed her intimately, while his eyes glowed with hot strong desire. For ages, they lay fiddling and fondling each other. They relaxed, locked together in a body embrace. He made no attempt to stick his tongue down her throat or his hand abruptly up her tunnel of love. He was content on this plateau of playfulness; now he was secure in the knowledge that he could penetrate her at will. This confidence allowed him to take his time, manipulating the pussy that was so prettily displayed under his nose. She stroked up and down the length of his penis; then scooped his hairy ball-sack into the palm of her hand. They continued making the lightest contact, with finger-tips only. Her fingers made a recce between his cheeks. Then back around his balls, until they encountered his gathering strength. He feather-fingered her fanny – no hard pulling or poking yet; just light deft strokes around her lust. She tickled his fancy and his cock.

Without warning, Peggy moved and spread Navek's legs wide apart. Taking a pot from the table beside the bed, she began to ladle sweetened, sticky milk on to his balls. She took a silver ladle from the pot – it was filled to the brim – and smoothed the thick substance on to his noble nuts. A twinge of conscience pricked her as she anointed this stud with Tom's exclusive sticky, dicky ointment. Quickly dismissing these thoughts, she watched fascinated as blobs of the white milk formed rivulets which ran in all directions. One wide river flowed through his thick forest and came to rest at the base of his stalk. Putting her tools to one side, she smiled and made ready to pick up his. With a quick movement, she tucked her long hair securely behind her ears. She went down on him, sucking his pubic hair into her mouth, drinking in all of the nectar. She licked around and around the root of his rod, which bobbed angrily and occasionally banged into her cheek. She ignored it and kept at her feast; sucking, licking, until his hair was squeaky clean. Only then did she attend to the very crux of the matter. Her tongue, hot as any furnace flame, shot wickedly around the base of his ever-thickening cock.

Slowly. Slowly.

The warm wet spear travelled up the pulsating path. When she reached the top, her tongue played in the tiny groove. First, she gnawed and nibbled one side until he could hardly bear her touch. Just when he thought he would explode, the prickling, passioned pinkie moved quickly around to the other side of his wonderful wand. She began a slow, gooley gobble as, inch by inch, his manhood disappeared into her moist, fiery mouth. She stopped when his balls hit her chin. Then, she started a tantalising milking of the long firm weapon. When she felt he was in danger of blowing his manhole cover, she drew back sharply. The steamy slug fell out into daylight. Peggy moved over on to her back; invitation in her eyes. Navek shifted his incredible hulk over her. She was dwarfed by his monster. Taking his weight on his arms, Navek positioned his cock, ready for the plunge in her pool. He lunged forward but bounced off her pearly portals. Exasperation made her moan. She reached down and took the cock in her two hands. Gingerly, she fed the beast to her starving snatch. He rode on down the randy road. Once he'd parked his long limo in her garage, he lay there luxuriating in her lap of lust. His body was rigid – absolutely still. But his cock beat incessantly on her drum. Her groin was in a fury. His breath was hot upon her face. She grasped his bum-cheeks firmly in her hands and pulled him even further into her. She could feel the heat of his cock tunnelling through her inner core. Navek moved and the whole weight of his body crushed into Peggy. He sensed her nipples, as sharp as needles, jabbing his bare chest. His body began to undulate as his uncooked joint skewered into her hungry hole. He rode on, pushing her from one orgasm to the next and still she begged for more. On, on, he went, until Peggy orgasmed into oblivion. Her senses dulled, her pussy raw, she blacked out on a giant wave of steamy sex. She finally descended from her climactic cloud to find him rock-hard and as randy as ever.

'Please come, darling,' Peggy begged of her new-found Superfuck.

With not a word, he moved his cock into top gear and broke the speed limit. A rush of come swept to the head of his cock and flooded into her.

The annoying jangle of the telephone rang out. Breathlessly, Navek grabbed it from its cradle and held it to Peggy's ear. She heard the pips, put her hand over the mouthpiece and said:

'I think it's Tom phoning from the pub!'

The coin dropped and the line was connected.

'Navek?' intoned a frightened voice on its last legs. 'Is that you?'

'Quick, quick,' said Peg, pushing the receiver at him, 'I think it's a distressed and crushed Violet.'

'What is it?' questioned Navek of the instrument.

'I'm in terrible trouble . . .'

The line went dead.

CHAPTER SIX

Whooray for Whorelicks

Peggy looked around at the faces of the customers in the public bar of the Green Man. The usual sprinkling of locals were there. A couple of bears drinking Hofmeister and a white stallion drinking Scotch. Frankenstein, refreshed all over, sat in one corner with Schubert, helping him with the unfinished symphony.

'Have you seen my housekeeper?' she asked of the jolly landlord behind the bar.

'No,' came the none-too-encouraging reply.

'Well, have you seen my husband Tom?'

'I've only been here a few weeks. He went back to his space station before I had a chance to meet him. What was he wearing?'

'Levis, a green T-shirt and sneakers.'

'Haven't seen him – the only green thing we've seen around here this evening was a little green monster. But I assumed he was with this lot,' he pointed at the bears, the horse and Frankenstein. 'I presumed he must have been from the film studios.'

Peggy's blood curdled in her arteries as she took in what he'd said. What if Violet got the serum from the drop, thought Peggy, and Tom deprived of his humanoid-giving juice, has reverted to his real alien self?

She turned from the landlord without a word and pushed her way through the imbibing bears to the pay phone in the lobby by the gents. No sign of Violet, nor Tom.

'The phone box!' she blurted out and fled the pub, leaving the host wide-eyed and Pegless.

She ran down the dimly-lit main street, screeched to a halt outside the telephone kiosk and tried to lever the door open with her finger nails. When she'd broken three nails on three non-doors, she managed to find what she was looking for and yanked the door wide open. What she saw made her heart stop short. There, on the concrete floor, lay Violet's string of simulated pearls – broken. Near it, lying with its face all cracked and smashed, her Mickey Mouse watch. Even as she stared at these effects, Peggy felt something wet and slimy slither over her hand which she'd rested against one of the panes of glass. She almost had a seizure as the green slime oozed a trail through her fingers and bounced off Violet's beads. It came to rest, menacingly, on the floor of the booth.

Wherever Violet was, she'd have to fend for herself now. Peggy's only thought was to return to Navek.

She fumbled in her shoulder bag for a coin, spilling the contents of the commodious container all over the floor of the phone box.

'Eureka,' she screamed as she found some small change.

She dialled her number with trembling fingers. She waited what seemed like hours for her connection. A click, and *Tom* answered the phone.

She spluttered a reply to his breezy hello: 'I . . . I . . . th . . . thought you were down here at the pub. I came across to find you.'

'No need for that, dear,' said Tom reassuringly. 'I just had a quick drink and I'm home again now. I can't understand how we missed each other. I've got the car so I'll nip across and pick you up. Wait for me on the lochside.'

A few minutes later, Peggy was standing with the water of the loch lapping around her wellies. The scene in front of her, once so comforting and familiar, now held only terror for the frightened girl. Even her home, atop the little isle, painted a sinister silhouette on the skyline. The hum of Tom's motor broke the stillness of the dark night. In the shadows, the sleek-nosed vehicle took on the shape of a woman-eating monster. It came swiftly towards her. Peggy shivered in her rubbers. She willed herself to stop trembling. She had to be calm and act normally. As the duck pulled in beside her, the door swung open and hubby flashed a toothy grin. As meek as a fly, she eased herself into the mechanical spider's web.

Tom leant across from his steering wheel and gave her a peck on the cheek. She steeled herself for an inhuman jelloid kiss, but was nonplussed by the warm earthy quality of this show of affection. She took a good look at the man on the seat beside her. The reflection of the headlights on the water floodlit his fine features. Could this fine, upstanding man really be the creature that lived in a jelly mould? At that moment, it could only be her Tom. Surely, this was all a dream from which she'd soon be awakened by her Prince Charming. Tom's voice broke through her silent musings.

'That was very sweet of you to come and look for me,' he lied, patting her knee affectionately. 'But you needn't have bothered. I just felt like getting out of the house for a while. You didn't mind, did you?'

Taken aback by this, Peggy managed to reply. 'I fancied a drink too. That was all. And I didn't want to be left alone with Navek, after he'd said all those things about you.'

'That's OK, Peggy. You needn't worry about him any more. His ankle got very quickly better and he left. I lent him a boat and he's gone. We'll have time for each other now. We'll be able to start the family we've both longed for.'

The thought of producing a clutch of jelly babies sent cold rivulets of fear up her spine. But she kept her cool and replied:

'Yes darling. Wonderful.'

Watching closely for any kind of reaction, she continued: 'We'll be completely alone. Violet went off without a word. I happened to look out of the window, to see her canoeing off towards the mainland at great speed, and with great dexterity in her paddles. Where can she have gone, do you think?'

She fixed an unwavering gaze upon her husband's profile.

There wasn't even a humanoid flicker of eyelid. 'I don't know,' he said, 'you employed the girl. You know what these locals are like. They're always nipping off for a bit of a jock [strap] on the side.'

The rest of the journey across the loch passed without incident and, when the pair reached their home, Tom was delighted by a new mood which overtook his Peg.

'You just pop upstairs,' she said. 'I'll be up in a moment. Go and take your clothes off, lie on the bed, relax and wait for me to come. I'm going to prepare my instruments of tort . . . I mean, pleasure,' said Peg, covering her little fluff with great aplomb. 'I'll just heat up the oils and warm the towels. You're going to the have the best massage of your life.' And the last, she thought to herself.

Tom walked up the stairs.

Peggy, realising that these were the only moments she'd have to herself, fled into the kitchen and rattled the pots. She had to get into that lean-to in this brief respite. She had to get hold of his serum and dispose of it. She had to alienate her husband for ever.

Quietly, she let herself out of the back door and scurried down the garden path under cover of the privet hedge. A quick examination of the heavy, well-secured door, told her she hadn't a hope in hell of getting in that way. Her only hope was a legover the ladder!

The steps leaned against the pear tree. Mustering all her strength, she dragged them across the garden and placed them in position against the side of the shed. Niftily, she mounted them. She scrambled across the slates and tried to force the skylight open.

It was firmly locked from inside and she could not budge it.

There's nothing for it, she thought, I'll have to smash the glass.

She placed a dainty latex-covered foot against the pane and pressed down. She kept applying pressure until she heard the sheet fracture. It was then a very simple task to push the glass in. She held her breath and waited for the crash. The glass tinkled to the floor. She glanced back towards the house, frightened that Tom may have heard. But all was quiet, so she jumped through the hole and into the shed. She swung herself down on to Tom's workbench. It was pitch dark. She felt her way off the bench and on to the floor. Her next move was to find the light switch. She put out a hand in front of her and groped her way across the shed. Her hand came into contact with something. Was this the switch? Strange . . . it felt long and warm and pulsating. Terror took her by the tits. Was this another of Tom's evil little aliens? A muffled scream came from the pulsating pole in her hand. She leapt back as warm sticky liquid seeped over her fingers. She fell against the wall of the hut and her shoulder knocked the switch. The room was bathed in electric light.

Her relief was exquisite. She'd had her hand on Navek's cock all the time! He was trussed like a chicken, gagged, and hanging from a harness hooked into the ceiling. Being no Houdini, he'd been unable to undo it. He was naked except for the decorative straps that held him in situ. Peggy acted quickly. She cut him down and whipped off his muzzle.

'Thank God you've relieved me,' he said with considerable humour, considering the situation.

'There's no time to lose,' said Peggy, taking him in hand again. 'Where's the serum?'

'Over there. Those Baby Bio bottles are full of it,' Navek said, pointing to a shelf above the bench.

'I can't stand here chatting all day.' And hurriedly Peggy filled him in. 'The monster awaits me. He's lying there, relaxing, and waiting to plant his evil seed in me. I'll go back and carry on – you get rid of the serum. Don't worry I won't let him fuck me. I've got a plan . . . and anyway I'm on the pill.'

Navek stopped her.

'No *you* chuck it down the waste disposal, then we're sure it's gone for good.'

'OK,' she agreed breathlessly, 'but make sure you keep an eye on the house tonight. Something could go wrong. I'll try to drug him. He usually has a cup of Whorelicks before he goes to bed. You leave a knockout pill in the kitchen. In the morning we'll decide how to dispose of him. I must get back now . . . '

Peggy planted a kiss on his pinkie, gathered up the Baby Bio bottles and let herself out of the shed. Back in the kitchen, she was just about to pour the serum down the drain, when Tom's voice floated urgently down the stairs.

'Where are you darling? Surely, the oil is boiling by now!'

'Be right there, Tom,' shouted Peggy.

Flustered, Peggy turned from the sink and hurried out of the kitchen. She was still clutching the bottles. She heard a creak of springs as Tom got out of bed. What could she do? The game was up. She would be discovered red-handed. Without hesitating, she chucked all six bottles upside down in the huge tub of earth which housed her indoor plants. The evil liquid gurgled from the containers and sank into the rich red earth, until no trace of it could be seen.

Retracing her steps, Peggy grabbed the pot of oil from the Aga – she'd put it there to warm – and took a bundle of warm towels from the airing cupboard in the hall. Clutching these to her, she bounded across the lounge and up the stairs. Tom was standing waiting for her – nude – his shape completely filling the door frame. Behind him, the bedroom was dimly illuminated by candlelight.

'Ah, there you are, I was wondering what you were getting up to.'

Tom's words brought fear to Peggy's pudenda and made her pubes stand on end.

'Just making sure the unguent is at the right temperature, Tom,' flustered Peggy, as she walked past him into the boudoir.

A hand gripped her shoulder and gently kneaded the back of her neck. She stood frozen to the spot as the hand explored the curvature of her buttock cheeks. Peggy turned to face Tom. Then:

'No, no, Tom, I don't want you to touch me. I want you to lie back on the bed and enjoy what I've got in store for you.'

Tom obeyed, propping himself up on the pillows, so he could see what she was doing.

First, Peggy draped the towels over the radiator to keep them warm. Then, she placed the bottle of sweet-smelling oil on the floor beside the heater. Standing at the foot of the ornate chintz-decked four-poster extravaganza, Peggy kicked off her wellies. She meandered over to the tape-deck and selected something loud and smoochy. The aural gratification allowed the freezing Navek to creep into the downstairs loo and don Tom's new sheepskin coat and woolly-lined space boots; while upstairs, Peggy was in full-twirl. She eased her black leather waistcoat from her shoulders and shrugged it to the floor. The buttons of her crisp, white embroidered cowboy shirt sought her attention next. As she popped a couple of the brass buttons, more and more of her creamy flesh was revealed to Tom's gaze.

'Hello, tits, long time no see,' said Tom unnecessarily.

Taking no notice of her husband, she started on her wide-cuffed, black leather gauntlets. She bit at each fingertip, and then slowly pulled each finger, coaxing the hide down and from her hands. As each glove came free, she tossed it playfully in the direction of the bed. She parted her legs, placed her hands on her hips and ground her crotch enticingly in time to the music. Her black stretch pants clung to her heavenly shape. Tom could plainly see the glorious crack of her pussy through the sheer material. Placing a finger in her open mouth, Peggy sucked on this surrogate cock and then swivelled slowly around, until the high, tight cheeks of her bottom confronted him. She moved her head and looked at him through a fringe of thick blonde tresses. With her other hand, she caressed the full curves of her arse. Slowly she traced a line with her hand from the deep valley of her bottom, up her slender back, and through her corn-coloured hair. She piled the thick tresses high on her head, then let them cascade back down again, over her shoulders. Turning her head away from him, she fiddled momentarily with the remainder of her buttons. Her two hands tugged the material from her belted waist. Peggy held out the shirt – like a kite – on either side of her body. She threw him a glance over her shoulder and pouted provocatively as she let the shirt fall from one shoulder. Gradually, she eased the shift further, until both her satin-skinned shoulders were bare. The blouse scooped down, revealing more and more of her flesh. A soft slither signalled the shirt's descent to the floor. Peggy was naked from the waist up. She stood there proud, upright; her back outlined against the pale green walls. The soft candlelight played upon her smooth, taut skin. The curves of her shoulders and backbone were accentuated by the flickering shadows of the spluttering light. It was a divine sight and Tom's stalk rose further from its pubic bed. Peggy could hear his raucous breathing, even above the amplified violins. She turned her head and shot a glance at her man.

Exactly where I wanted, she thought. Things are going according to plan. I'll only have to touch him and he'll explode. Then he won't be able to plant any foreign bodies in me!

So thinking, she crossed her arms and squashed her breasts to her. Peggy did a slow full circle, giving Tom a brief glimpse of her succulent goodies. With her back to him once again, she dropped her arms; then, half turned, giving him a glimpse of one ripe melon decorated by a glace cherry. Inch by inch, she fingered her way up over her haunch and cupped a beautiful breast in her palms. Her eyelids fluttered – almost closed – as she lowered her head and raised a noble nipple to her open mouth. Her tongue moistened her lips before they closed over the bud. Her lips pouted and posed as she teased the organ-stop erect. Sighing, she let the nipple fall from her mouth, swivelled around and sucked in the other rubbery teat. As soon as the brown stalk had been teased to perfection, she freed it from her rosebud mouth and turned to face her husband full-on. She stood there brazenly, staring straight into Tom's narrow slits of lust.

The corner of her lips lifted as she whispered: 'You'll have to wait for it. I'm not ready yet . . .'

With these words, she began her mammary masturbation, teasing and pulling at her pert, young breasts. They bounced and bobbed in her fingers as she applied pressure to the ripe plums. Tiring of this juggling act, her hands slithered down to the chunky buckle of her leather belt. She gripped the end of the hide thong, unbuckled it, and whipped it out from the loops. The leather strap came free and Peggy twirled it menacingly around in front of her. The lasso whistled as she thrashed the air. With a smile, she let go and the belt sailed through space and landed on the canopy above the bed. It hung down like a cobra, only inches from Tom's head. Peggy tugged at the fastening at the top of her trousers, snapped it open and gripped the tab of her zip. Tooth by tooth, she lowered the metal fly. Tom propped himself up in readiness for the indecent exposure. But Peggy wasn't finished yet. Noticing Tom's eager movements, she pulled the zip up again, after allowing him only the briefest glimpse of her blonde curls. She about-turned and gave him full-sighted benefit of her cheeks. The material strained to cover the swelling hillocks of bumflesh. She put her hands down, unzipped her trousers again and pushed her arms inside. Teasingly, she inched the material down until the dark crack of her bottom came into view. Swiftly, Peggy freed herself of the clinging garment. With her back to Tom, she mounted the armchair at the foot of the bed. She raised her bottom and lowered her head, peeking at her husband through her pubic fringe. Tom got more and more turned on, as he surveyed the high smooth buttocks and long lissom legs of his Peg. She jiggled her bum before his very eyes and fingered the deep secretive crevice between her legs. Suddenly, she spun around and, before he could take in a full-frontal view, leapt at him. The bedsprings creaked as she landed astride his reclining form.

'Turn,' she commanded.

The jolly green giant flipped bum up in the quilt and his dick dug deep into the duckdown. Peggy grabbed the bottle of warm oil and flicked open the cap. She squirted a long, long stream of oil along Tom's vertebrae. She watched fascinated as the white liquid formed a lake in the well of his back. He shuddered deliciously as the warm unguent spilled on to his rear. Peggy dipped her fingers in the pool of orange-scented balm and spread it upwards and out over his broad, manly shoulders. She massaged his clavicles, rubbing the oil purposefully into his pores. She moved on and upwards, taking his neck in her two hands, and applied pressure to either side, just under his ears. Her manipulations almost made him suffocate in the feathers. His cock was not in danger of suffocation, however – it was drilling its way niftily through the bedclothes and on into the mattress. Like a breast-stroker easing her way through water, Peggy moved down her lover's body. The sweeping movements enabled her to cover the whole of Tom's broad back. As she pummelled him, she lowered herself on to the rounded curves of his buttocks. Tom felt her fruit bruise a cheek. She fingered her way up his vertebrae and as she stretched out her arms, Tom was aware of her proud flesh bearing down on him. Her papillae furrowed into his taut frame. Peggy slid seductively down from her perch on his rump and kneeled astride his legs. Her hands heaved to his hunkers. She pressed her two thumbs together, fanned her fingers and ground away at his coccyx. Her digits dabbled in his foothills. Then she was off. She pummelled his inner thigh; an electric charge shot up his right leg. His brown, green/yellow and blue terminals fused as the thunderbolt shocked his lower body. He wished he'd been earthed! Peggy moved her attentions to his other leg, causing a similar electric storm. His lightning conductor jerked wildly under the strain of the girl's ten thousand volt touch. Her nails scraped playfully in the thick undergrowth which grew in abundance on the backs of his legs. Her touch became softer, until she was merely teasing the tufts of hair. These gentle fumblings ruffled the roots of his feathery down. All at once, the wind changed. Hot breath hit the hollow at the base of his spine. Then, a moist tongue was upon him. The tapir licked lovingly along the curvature of his rear. Around and around his flesh moons it dallied and then stabbed at his fur-trimmed canyon. A human being would have been beyond control by now, but Tom was no ordinary mortal. No mortal, at all, in fact. Anyone else, would have turned to jelly!

Peggy took him by the shoulders and heaved him over on to his back. She was terrified by the monster proportions of his rampant cock. It stood stock-still, upright and almost bursting at the seams. She anointed its head with a thick dollop of steamy cream. Contact! He quivered as the globule wobbled dangerously on his fleshy knob. It avalanched down his pink pastures. Peggy watched fascinated as the goo oiled the sides of his monstrous erection. Without warning, she lunged. Tom sucked in his breath as her hands fastened around his slimy slug. His member squelched rudely under her organ pumping. Up and down she slithered, as the ruthless rudder grew in width and stature. She pumped the pulsating prodder for all she was worth, keeping both hands firmly around the beast. The oily substance seeped through her fingers and splashed messily over Tom's stomach and thighs. As she continued her slurpings, his breath came in short, deep pants. The head of his cock bulged as the inner pumpings in his scrotum began their work. The culmination of his climax clawed its way up his cock. Tom raised his buttocks from the bed and his muscles rippled in ecstasy as he threw himself into the finale of this fuck.

With relief, Peggy saw the droplets of come wend their way down his wand. She fell beside him, exhausted by her labours without love. They snuggled together and it wasn't long before Tom dropped off to sleep. She lay there listening to his deep regular breathing. It would now be safe to move, she thought.

Peggy eased herself away from Tom's outstretched arm and edged gingerly off the bed. She was halfway across the room to the door, when Tom sat bolt upright.

'Where are you going?' he asked.

'I couldn't sleep,' she replied, 'I was going down to get myself a nice hot cup of Whorelicks. D'you want one?'

'What a good idea!' rejoined Tom.

Peggy passed out of the door and ran down the stairs to the kitchen. She was busying herself with cups and saucers when Navek let himself in the back door. Peggy put a finger to her lips.

'He's still awake. Be careful.'

Navek pressed a pill into the palm of Peggy's hand.

'It's a bit too late for birth control!' she joked.

'Put this in his hot drink,' ordered Navek. 'It'll knock

him out cold. And then we will be able to see exactly what we're battling against. As soon as the effects of the serum wear off, his atoms will regroup in alien form. Go quickly.'

As Peggy crossed the hallway, she was too preoccupied with her own personal problems to notice the activity taking place in the large plant pot, where she'd so carelessly loosed Tom's potion.

She bounded up the stairs, put the two cups of night drink on the table by the bed and moved to get the hot towels that were draped on the radiator. As she plucked them from the heater, she momentarily turned her back on Tom. She did not see her alien lover perform a very dexterous conjuring trick. He switched the beakers and began sipping the harmless drink. Peggy came back to the bed and wrapped him in a cocoon of hot towels. She snuggled down beside him and drank her draught...

She was awoken some hours later, by a clammy green tendril which was creeping across her face. She was so terrified that she could only open one eye; and that only very cautiously. She shut it again quickly! Her bedroom had turned mouldy. It seemed to be full of thick green smog. Her first thought was that this was Tom's proper form. And it had taken over the entire house! Slowly, Peggy, still stiff with fright, raised her lids. All about her, and all over her, grew long green fronds of vegetation. They criss-crossed her body in a restraining spider's web. She was bound, but not gagged, to the bed.

'Tom,' she whispered tentatively, thinking that perhaps she could reason with the green tangle on her tits. 'The game is up. I know it's you.'

She put on a brave face which she really didn't feel, and continued talking to the plant, in the hope that it would find a drop of human kindness in its leaves.

'Please let me go,' she whimpered.

Her soft dulcet tones did nothing to stop the plant's

growth. It grew steadily up towards her throat. Her blood ran cold as the wisps of green closed around her. A particularly cheeky chappie branched forth between her legs. A new shoot tried to push its way between her lower portals. She was desperate. Realising that argument was futile – and not being sure whether it was Tom or not – Peggy realised that she'd have to yell for help. And take whatever assistance – alien or otherwise – came to her aid. She opened her mouth to scream but a large insistent leaf smothered her cry of help. What now?

In the nick of time, Peggy remembered her make-up bag. It was on the bedside table. Could she reach it in time? With all her might, she forced an arm through the tunnel of greenery. Inch by inch, her hand crept closer to the table. Her nails scratched at the wooden surface. One more attempt brought her fingers closer. Her nails rasped against the material of the case. She strained further until she got finger and thumb around the zip tab. With baited breath, she carefully pulled the bag towards her. She misjudged the width of the table. The bag fell as it reached the edge. Her heart stopped. She was convinced the bag would fall from her grasp. But, with a supreme effort, she managed to hold on to it. It swung perilously in the gap as she mustered all her strength to pull it up and on to the bed. She couldn't move. She rested for a moment. Sweat was now breaking freely from her brow. She moved her hand around and under the bag and, with a flick of her wrist, threw it over to the other side of her body. Her other hand, also, trapped alongside her, groped around furiously until it found the bag. Clumsily, it fumbled with the fastening. Finally, it had the zip open and felt inside the purse. Peggy's fingers closed on an assortment of useless objects. Then her little finger wormed its way into one of the metal rings of her manicure scissors. Gently, the finger pulled the scissors free. Once they were out, she got a proper hold on them. She stabbed viciously at the willowly green constrictions around her body. The plant writhed as she continued her assault on its foliage. The severed ends shrunk back and soon she was out of its horrible clutches. Appalled, she sat up on the bed and surveyed the rapacious vegetable. It clung to everything. It grew up the walls, over the framework of the four-poster, dripped from the ceiling, blocked the light from the window and filled the doorframe with its evil plant growth. There was nothing for it, she would have to machete her way out with her manicure scissors! The monstrous herb didn't appear to be harmful – just full of jolly green life. Even as she watched, its botanic arms fought their way into the room.

She made to get up and a tight band of pain encircled her head. The searing stab of agony blinded her. She sat back, clutching her forehead. What *had* happened to her? The last she remembered was drinking her Whorelicks. And slipping Tom his. What can have gone wrong? The only explanation likely was that she'd got the wrong drink. She surely couldn't have drugged herself by mistake . . . The clever alien must have switched the cups. And if this green stuff wasn't him, then where was he? And what was he? And where was that useless Navek? Anger overtook her. What the hell was *he* playing at? Another thought struck her. Perhaps the plants had already claimed him as their first victim. Or worse – had Tom eliminated him? But first things first, she must get out of the house.

With a blood-curdling cry, she flung herself into the tentacles of green. Hacking away with the small pair of bent scissors, she managed to cleave a path to the door. She gazed in horror at what used to be the stairway. It was now a jungle of creeping ivy. Bravely, she tusselled with the stalks. Tread by tread and snip by snip, she fought her way through the thicket. Down the stairs she went. At the bottom, she saw the root of her problem. Her dear, wee houseplants had gone berserk. The whole house had been taken over by the horticultural display. She sat on the bottom step and laughed like a drain as realisation dawned. It was the serum! It had turned her fragile saplings into a herbaceous boarder! It would be paradise for David Bellamy . . .

Enough of this floricultural rambling, she thought.

And with not another thinks, she battled her way across the hall and fell out of the front door. The sight in front of her fair took her breath away. It was one of those unearthly Scottish mornings. Bands of mist floated above the glassy smooth water of Loch McCock. Shafts of sunlight streamed through the haze and spilled on to the grateful soil. Peggy forgot her troubles as she basked in the romantic beauty of that Hibernian morn. The scent of the heather, the smell of the flowers. The gentle aromatic breeze carried nature's bouquet to her. A crash from the shed brought her chronic situation brutally back. Had that been a human or inhuman crash, she wondered. There was only one way to find out . . .

She thrust her bare feet into the spare pair of boots which Violet had left in the porch, circled the house, and took off down the garden path as naked as nature intended. Stealthily, she wellied her way to the back of the wooden structure. The ladder was still there – where she'd left it. As she mounted the first rung, her heart thudded uncomfortably in her breast. She put all her weight on to the ladder, lifted her other foot off the ground and began her climb. Slowly, carefully, she made her ascent. When her head was level with the skylight, she stopped. Tremulously, she peeked through the broken window. On the floor lay a bundle of rags. It looked like Navek. A movement at the other end of the shed caught her eye. She wormed her way up another rung, curiosity creeping up her crotch. The wooden bar on which she stood snapped like a breadstick. Her hands slithered over the grey slates, as Peggy tried to get a grip on her precarious situation. She scrabbled wildly for the guttering but her scratched fingers failed to connect. She fell like a stone into a wheelbarrow full of thistles. Dazed, she lay there, unaware of the green hand which, at that very moment, was turning the key of the shed door. It creaked open and an amorphous shape flowed out . . .

CHAPTER SEVEN

Star Whores

'Ten . . . Nine . . . Eight . . . Seven . . . Six ... Five . . . Four . . . Three . . . Two . . . One . . . We have lift-off . . . '

Fatman's voice rang out in the control room of the probe-ship. Robinski looked with golly-gosh eyes at her hero; taking command yet again.

The couple were strapped into high-backed tailor-made leather chairs. The craft zoomed away from earth and into sonicspace.

Robin had been slightly dazed by the speed with which Fatman had propelled her from the office to Archangelskoye, a pretty hamlet on the outskirts of Moscow. They'd driven through snow-covered forests on Fatty's supersonic sledge. On the way, her consort had treated her to a night in the luxurious summer palace of Count Yusopf, which had been taken over by the CGB as a holiday home for overworked agents.

It had been Robin's first visit to this palatial watering hole and she had been amazed as Fatman had shown her around the vast mansion. At the doorway, they were required to place overshoes on their feet so they wouldn't damage the highly-polished floors. The vast, high main doors opened into a gracious entrance hall the size of a football pitch. She was shown all the beautiful and priceless antiques which were crammed into the dozens of princely rooms on the ground floor. But the thing that caught Robinski's eye most of all was a bed .... No ordinary bed this, but a quite magnificent example. Its canopy was attached to the lofty ceiling and cascaded down almost forty foot to end in a cloud of spun gold around the bedhead.

'This is our room,' Fatman had said, bouncing on the bed in glee.

Robinski's eyes had widened in wonder. She joined Fatman on the soft, giving, feather mattress. Soon they'd be naked and under the covers. A discreet knock at the door heralded the arrival of Gladys, a small round robot.

'Supper, master,' said the metallic slave.

Gladys was not in her prime; she had seen better robotic days. Her metal head resembled a tin hat which had been through the wars ... the mill and the mangle. Two eyes like fried eggs peeked out at the world from the brim of her hat-head. Her stumpy body looked as though it had been made from somebody's old colander. Legs like drainpipes finished off this mechanical wonder.

As Gladys surveyed the scene of lust in front of her, her head did a three hundred and sixty degrees turn in embarrassment. When it had finally settled in its rightful place on her shoulders, she sailed forth across the room and creaked to a halt by the side of the bed. Her metal claws clutched a small tray on which was placed a demi-carafe of vodka, two shot glasses, a bowl of caviare, slices of lemon and a couple of spoons. She placed the tray on the bedside table and trundled off.

Fatman, taking on the role of mother, poured the vodka and told Robinski to get stuck into the caviare. They snorted vodka and stuffed caviare until every black ball and every drop of fiery liquid had gone.

With no more ado, Fatman was upon her. He hammered

his sickle inside her and took her in an extraordinary burst of lust. He was rough. He was tough. He bruised her. And this extraordinary treatment made her feel even more randy than normal. He fucked her harder than he'd ever fucked her before. And she responded to the friction of his pumping. The beast in him brought out the beast in her. Fur flew, mouths bit, and nails scratched, as he ravaged and ravaged her. It was like being had by Hannibal *and* his elephants. They exploded together. Robinski lay bashed and battered as Fatman collapsed into sleep.

Next morning, they breakfasted quickly, climbed into the front of his Zil and bundled Gladys in the back. The robot sat uneasily on the edge of her seat. Her head rotated erratically as Fatman careered sideways on the icy roads towards the airbase to the north of Archangelskoye. The spacefield looked spooky in the thin morning light. Odd shapes rose from the snow. The trio headed for the oddest shaped one of all. They were chatting gaily and didn't notice the dark-haired slim girl who slipped after them aboard their craft. If the top agent Fatman had been more observant, he would have noticed a familiar glint of gold behind the ruby lips of Iva Knockabollockoff.

'What the fuckski are we up to now?' enquired Binski from her high-back space chair in front of the huge control panel hanging down from the ceiling. 'You never tell me anything! Why am I always kept in the dark,' she nagged.

Fatman completed his after-lift-off checklist and eased his chair back on its runners.

'I got through to Tom at last, early this morning. Things have gone radically wrong at McCock. The serum that I arranged to be dropped was picked up by Navek's assistant, Violet Tree, and Tom had to eliminate her. His wife is now convinced that he is, in fact, an alien. She tried to drug him but failed. Unfortunately, she had already poured away all of his serum. So, he is in his normal green jelloid form, with no way of taking on human shape. We must help him. At least, he's captured Navek. But we have to get him some more serum. That's where we're going now – I've got a load of the stuff in a secret space hideaway. It'll take about eighteen hours to get there and back. I know it's risky to leave Tom that long. But there's nothing else I can do. The last lot I sent him was enough for months. I couldn't leave the rest in Moscow – it's far too dangerous. I'm already taking a big enough risk conducting my sperm tests at home. I'm sure I'm watched and followed, twenty-four hours a day. The only peace I get is when I'm in space.'

Hidden in a ventilation shaft between the control room and staff canteen, Iva Knockabollockoff smiled to herself as she recorded every word on her wristwatch tape machine. Mr Big had sent her to uncover Fatman's plot. Little did he know she was on the other side.

Meanwhile, Gladys the robot, on her first day trip to space, and not being *au fait* with in-flight procedure, trundled forth in search of a cuppa. Her magnetic wheels stopped her from floating into the air. The ship had no gravity. She wheeled her way to the canteen. The steel doors parted smoothly at her approach. She rattled on the doorstep and then rolled over the threshold. With considerable difficulty, she got herself on to a high stool at the counter and waited for service. The Waitrobot, who looked remarkably like a cast-off from the Wizard of Oz, oiled his way up to her and his metallic voice boomed out:

'I'm sorry, but we don't serve robots in here.'

'That's all right,' chirped Gladys, 'I don't eat them!'

Gladys saw stars but not out of the porthole. The cafe's tin person had fetched her an unkind blow with its pincer-like claws. Her eyeballs shot up and disappeared under the jaunty brim of her head. When she came electronically to, she was flying towards the metal doors. They swished open, she sailed through and smashed into the wall on the other side of the corridor.

These modern robots have no sense of humour, she thought to herself.

She stood there, rattling her tin with fury. She didn't hear the approach of another old-timer. R-T Far-T came around the corner at great speed and almost crashed into the wobbling suit of armour that was Gladys.

They looked into each other's eyes. Gladys' huge feathery eyelashes fluttered bashfully under Far-T's bold stare. Her tin turned a tasteful tomato red under his obvious scrutiny. A large red heart on a metal cantilever arm shot out from the robot's tin torso. It flashed and pulsated on the end of its pole. Their microphonic ears heard the tinny scraping of violins. They fell hopelessly in love.

Far-T tried desperately to get his legover but couldn't raise either foot an inch from the floor because of the magnetism. With a clank, he sat down, motioning Gladys to do the same. He busied himself with their knobs and eventually switched off their electric current; so, fusing their magnets. The now-weightless metal lovers floated to the ceiling. They disappeared down the walls of the corridor, arm-in-aluminium-arm.

Back on the flight-deck, Fatman floated around the central console, explaining the intricate controls to an awed Robinski.

'Golly, gosh,' said Binski, gazing proudly at her many-faceted Fatty.

Binski was enthralled by the circular control room. It was a bubble of clear plastic. Through it, in whatever direction she looked, she could plainly see the dark, velvet blanket of space. This murky curtain was relieved only, by a million pinpoints of light. Other worlds . . . She could see, off to the side, the tiny ball of the receding earth. Still visible, were the familiar shapes of the continents. They were travelling away from it at seven hundred times the speed of light. Soon it would be completely lost to view, and a feeling of space isolation would overtake them. But she was with her Fatty, and he knew no fear!

'This is the light-drive control,' said a proud Fatman, as he moved around the console gripping on to the grabrails. His feet floated gracefully behind him.

He went on to show her all his knobs and switches, explaining the uses of the vast bank of controls and flashing lights. Then, he moved on to the monitoring system – curved screens above the controls, sunk into the central superstructure. He was showing Robinski how it worked; how he could flash to any part of the ship. He punched several buttons and a picture flashed on above them. It was R-T Far-T's bedchamber. It was furnished in the period – early-space. A small, padded, gilded sleep-cage was where the little chappie slept. Gold and silver scatter cushions, covered the floor, ceiling and walls. Fatman noticed a glint of steel on the ceiling and zoomed in to get a closer look. Far-T and Gladys were hard at it; rogering like only robots can. Fatty flicked the audio switch and the speaker crackled into life. The clash of metal skin against metal skin reverberated around the control deck.

'Sounds like a couple of skeletons copulating on a tin roof in the rain! R-T!' boomed Fatman, 'stop farting about.'

The scatter cushions parted around the lovers and four bewildered eyes peered out at the camera.

'Come up here at once,' barked Fatman. 'I need you on the control deck immediately.'

As Fatman switched off the video, Robinski caught a glimpse of the scurrying mechanicals making for the door.

It seemed to Robinski that they'd only left earth minutes before, but already they'd picked up thirty gallons of serum from Fatty's hidey-hole of a spaceship and were, at that very moment, returning earthwards and bound for Scotland.

Fatty set the controls to automatic-astronaut and beckoned his beauty below. They lowered themselves down the companionway, gripping on to the sides with their hands and feet. They made their way, slowly, to Fatty's stateroom-with-a-view. This large area had windows on the universe. Fatty proudly pulled back the drapes which were fastened top and bottom of the windows. Robinski gasped for the second time that day as she took in the view afforded by the vast bay window.

She floated around the room ooohing and aaahing over the sumptuous soft furnishings, bolted to the floor.

'It's lovely,' said Robinski.

'So are you,' oiled Fatman, as he attempted to drift her way.

Robinski knew the look in his eye meant that his sap was rising and they were in for a fun time. She'd never had a weightless fuck and looked forward immensely to learning his technique. It was as he lunged towards her and missed completely, that she realised he had no technique at all. Eventually, Fatty did manage to get to grips with the girl. His arms encircled her waist and he held her to him as he released her silky chemise from the waistband of her skin-tight trousers. The material filled like a hot air balloon. Binski raised her arms and it drifted off over her head and away. Fatty undid the buttons of her fly and helped her down with her trousers.

'Leave your knickers on,' he begged.

The pervert fell to it with passion. He poked his fingers under the elastic of her knickers and pulled them until the crotch bit viciously into the tops of her legs. He could see her pubic hair bushing out either side of her panties. He spun her around and pulled the transparent black material tight across her behind. He could see every contour of her bottom. The full moons were split down the middle by a secretive crack. He stroked and rubbed her through the gauze, until her juices drenched the narrow strip of pantie cloth. Occasionally, a milky pearl escaped the knicker prison and drifted happily up, up and away.

The dual sensation of floating weightless and being fingered through her undies pushed Robinski to a heightened intensity of sexual stirrings. She was stirred like never before, by this large wooden spooner. But her lover had more tricks up his boilersuit than a magician has up his sleeve.

She turned to see him fumbling with his suit. Waiting for a white dove to appear from the folds, she was surprised when Fatty produced a long, straight cane. It whistled out of his pocket and landed on her upturned cheek. Binski winced.

'You've been a very naughty girl, shoving your bush through your knickers and opening your cheeks. You don't know who could be watching out there,' he said, pointing at his window. 'Any old alien could be looking at you. I'm going to have to punish you for the way you've behaved.'

Fear and delight took her in their turmoil. She stared wide-eyed at this display of viciousness.

Fatso narrowed his eyes, grit his teeth and puffed with exertion and ecstasy as he thwacked her thighs. One after another, the blows rained down on her near-naked buttocks. A criss-cross pattern of angry red weals appeared on her botty. The sight of them drove Fatty further and further towards his own alternative planet – a Saturn of sex. Binski tensed her bottom in preparation for more instant whip. But Fatty had thrown his cane away.

Looking her straight in the eye, Fatman said:

'I'm going to fuck you. Get those knickers off . . .'

Leaving her to struggle out of her undies, Fatty turned his attentions to his boilersuit. He'd got the knack of this, all right, because within seconds his fetching yellow spy's uniform bulged full of air. It looked as if Fatty was still in it, as it drifted up to the ceiling. He turned towards his loved one with a smile, only to find a black cloud of net descending over his face. Robinski's knickers were upon him and his wildest dream fulfilled. Fatty was a secret knickersniffer. As the wispy web spun around his face, his nostrils quivered at the smell of her.

His cock reared up as he savoured this heady cocktail. He drew deep draughts of her wonderful sex-sauce into his lungs. He wheezed like a diver returning to the surface. Having had his fill, he brushed her frillies aside and advanced upon his paramour. She was lying face-down with her back to the ceiling. He dived upwards towards her, attempting to come to rest face to face with her. But the pervert slightly misjudged his leap and his ankles whizzed either side of her face, while he travelled on along the ceiling. Regaining his composure, he scrabbled back to her. In an effort to steady his bulk – as he hovered beneath her – Robin grabbed him by the nipples. He screeched painfully to a halt and slapped her hands away. She took hold of where his waist should have been and pulled him to her. He attempted his first stab. He missed by a mile, his cock bounced, and Fatman glanced off her left boob at a right angle. This boob blow winded him as he wended floorwards. From his prone position on the floor, Fatman narrowed his sights on her honey-hole. Taking hold of his engorged member, he lifted off from the floor and flew to his fancy-pants. Robinski, seeing his approach, stretched her legs as wide apart as possible, to give the flying flotsam a larger-than-large target. The bobbling bolt bounced around the fleshy edges of her passion flower. After a few unsure fumblings, it slotted home. Fatman grabbed Robinski, squeezing her tightly to him. The two lay, impaled together, in mid-space. The gravitation had gone from his goolies. He began a weightless undulating fuck. The couple became a floating sextopus. Their arms and legs waved in slow motion and looked like the tendrils of a sea anemone. They floated around and up and down, gently nudging the walls, ceiling and floor as their fluid fuck culminated. His sputnik spunked, as her climax came . . .

They hung there and were soon asleep, enjoying wonderful weightless dreams. Neither of them heard the warning klaxon that rung out over the ship. It signified that the time was approaching for Commander Fatman to take over the controls. Their re-entry point was nigh. But the dreamers dreamed on. On the flight deck, Fatman's number two, Mr Spik, quivered in his spaceboots as he watched the ship sail past its re-entry point. All he could see on the screen above him – after he'd punched up the image from Fatman's stateroom – was an enormous 'Do Not Disturb' sign. It would be more than his life-force was worth to disobey this command.

'You stupid fart,' screeched the acrobatic Robin.

Fatman came around to find himself sailing towards the floor. Bleary-eyed and heavy with sleep, the boss bounced off the floor, wondering if this was freak in-flight turbulence. He zoomed ceilingwards again, only to be batted down once more by the angry Mongolian.

'You've missed our re-entry point, dope!' she exclaimed. 'Now we'll have to go around again!'

Retrieving his floating boilersuit and deck shoes, the person-in-control quickly donned them and searched frantically around for his captain's cap. Absent-mindedly, he plucked Robin's knickers from the ceiling and shoved these over his head. Binski couldn't believe her eyes – or his. They stared at her through the legholes.

Sniffing, he sailed from the room.

The wonder-woman could *not* believe this passing of the pervert. She lay sighing on the ceiling. Her reflections turned to Fatman's strange sniffings. The man was really quite a mess. For the first time in their short passionate relationship, she wondered if she was on the right side. Perhaps she should be with the goodies; perhaps she should be on the side of law and order. She had serious doubts as to whether Fatman could pull anything off. Except his cock! He seemed to blunder his way from disaster to disaster . . .

She gathered up her clothes and sloped off to her own

maisonette in the sky. Iva Knockabollockoff had watched their smutty proceedings with distaste. During her time as a double agent she had seen many things. Her one thought now was to touch-down and find out if Navek was still alive. But she could use this extra time usefully. In Moscow she had nosed into Robin's files and had found that the slim girl had a history of dissent and lesbianism. Fatman had, in fact, been her only male lover. Now she was clearly upset and disgruntled with the fat, foolish villain. Iva would act swiftly. Maybe she could move in for a quick kiss and kill.

Clambering down from her perch in the ventilation system, she made her way to the women's quarter. There, she hunted for Binski's room. But before she could find it, she heard the strains of a Mongolian folk-tune coming from the shower. Perfect! She followed the noise to the stark white shower-room. Binski luxuriated in her washbag of suds.

Iva, new to weightless space travel, was impressed by Fatman's ingenuity but not his intelligence. Surely, it would have been easier to have solved the ship's gravitational problems, than to have been forced to invent so many different devices, in order that his crew could live a more-or-less normal life? Putting her clothes in a locker, Iva unzipped one of the voluminous hanging shower bags. She stepped into it and fastened the zip at the front, all the way to her neck. Her body was now completely encased in plastic. Next to her, Robinski hummed a merry tune as she splashed it on all over. Iva had read the instructions to the shower. They were on a small plate on the wall. She had already programmed the bag to give her a shower, then a soap, then an oil, then a rinse and a hot air dry. The machine clicked into action and the pipes, which were attached to the suit, gurgled as fine jets of water sprayed on to her flesh. One particularly powerful jet kept hosing the top of her thighs. She moved fractionally and positioned herself so that the warm stream of water scored a bullseye on her genital target. She glanced across at her showering companion and, from the rhapsodic expression on her face, guessed that she was getting the same treatment.

Binski was throwing back her head and opening her legs to accommodate the hot jet. It was a jumbo! The force of the searing shaft of water parted her pink lips and geysered its way inside. She let out a growl. Iva could see the shadowy shape of her hands busy at her crotch. The sight of this water-wank made her crumpet quiver. Soon, *her* hands drifted down to assist the hot jet's penetration. She opened her banana split and her cherry got the full force of the water-pistol. Both girls were now in a watery heaven. They moaned in unison, as their hands delved deeper into their open beavers. Their heads turned and their eyes met through the escaping steam. The message was plainly clear. This was a time when girl needed girl. Binski's hot water bottle had now drained and balmy air was fanning her fan. The rush of wind to her breasts made her nipples stand like stilts. Iva could see this was a very turned-on tart. Breathing heavily, Robinski unzipped her shower-bag and floated out. The athletic maiden moved in on the still-captive hag-in-a-bag! She kissed her mouth, tàking long deep draughts. Iva's legs parted company. A leak of lust joined the droplets of oil that were now streaming, in a fine spray, all over her luscious body. Her nipples had hard-ons. They became as stiff as Robin's starch. Binski's tongue slid around Iva's mouth. The interminable kiss continued as the water programme finished its circle. Hot air caressed her curves. Binski's hand flew to the zip and peeled the ripe fruit out of its plastic shell. Out Iva floated, like a lustrous pearl from a gnarled oyster.

Binski stepped back to lap up the sight of the tantalising ladybird. She clung to the handrail at her side. She'd not seen this crew-member before. Recruitment was doing a much better job these days . . . this tasty morsel was a vast improvement on the usual beefy Russian peasant they employed. Robin was captivated by her beauty. Iva's usually fine features had been further softened by her recent fumblings. Her eyes were two languid pools of purple. Her mouth was full and her lips naturally magenta. Her unblemished skin glowed with health and vigour. Robinski sank to her knees and buried her head in the sweet-smelling thicket of her new-found lover. Iva clasped the sleek smooth head to her and lips met lips in a first intimate kiss. Iva lowered herself until she came face to face with Robin. They both clung to the hand-straps anchored in the floor and gazed into each other's eyes. With their free hands, they stroked and caressed and touched. With a balletic movement, Binski lowered her head to the other's breast and sucked in a crimson ruby. She chewed and nibbled on the proferred nut, while her hand massaged the full fleshiness of the other's globes. Iva let go her hold and floated up a few feet. Binski lay prone against the floor under her. Iva came to rest inches from the other girl and hovered over her face. Letting go, Binski slowly floated up towards the double agent. Her arms snaked around the other's firm thighs. Her fingers bit into the malleable flesh, while her tongue acquainted itself with the silky halo of curls at her crotch. The probe pushed deep into the vegetation and licked the whole of the hairy mound. At once, it made contact with the proferred perfect pink button. She tongued her way to the inner walls of Iva Knockabollockoff. Her pointed spear snuck in and out. She probed the fleshy folds of the petals that surrounded this flower. The blossom opened wide and offered the busy bee a taste of its honey. Drops of nectar ran down into Binski's mouth. Their closely-linked bodies were shaken by the same pleasure. Robin stroked and kneaded Iva's buttocks. The top-bitch curved and bent her hips incessantly. She pushed her body forward to enable the gleaming, wet, mouth organ further access inside her. It was sucked into her pussy like a tasty morsel of food. An unexpected, unearthly happiness filled the two women, as the spaceship rocketed towards its re-entry point for the second time that space-day.

Binski lowered a hand to her own well-oiled crevice. With an extreme lightness of touch, she investigated the raspberry ripple. She let her tongue slip from Iva's pink heaven and squeezed two fingers into the glorious gash. This movement caused her body to rise from the floor until she was lying horizontally, at crotch level to her lover. She felt Iva's tight muscles close juicily around her digits. She flipped, she flew, she flooded. Her two hands worked in perfect harmony on the two honeypots. She opened her eyes wide and drank in the length of her lover's body. It was topped by two firm, rounded breasts. Robinski, with such pleasure in both hands, started to blast off. Her movements became more rapid and frenzied, as she jerked them both on to a high plateau of new joys and delights.

A tremor from the ship's retro-rockets brought the girls back from their orgasmic orbit. They were entering the earth's gravitational pull. Even as Robinski pulled her hands from their sex sockets, things were beginning to happen in the ship. For a start, Iva was gently falling to the floor. So were other things . . .

Gradually, the falling objects settled in to their proper place and the world loomed nearer.

Binski, realising that she'd soon be needed on the bridge, rose. She bent and gave the new woman in her life one last long lingering kiss. Then she was nought but a clatter of spaceboots in the distance. Iva donned her suit and crawled back into her hiding place in the ventilator system. The gold of her teeth glinted through the grill . . .

Flushed, Robinski ran into the control room and flung her arms around a scowling Fatty.

'Strap yourself in,' said the humourless commander. 'We'll be touching down in ten minutes.'

Luton Airport loomed large on the horizon.

'Look,' said Fatty, 'Inverness Airport.'

'But there's no sea!' exclaimed his sidekick.

'Yes, there is,' said the know-all, pointing a finger at a small reservoir in the distance way below.

Binski didn't want to argue. She'd let him find out for himself. She chuckled maliciously.

Inside Luton's control tower, another normal Monday morning was in full swing. But not for long. Efficient air traffic controllers spoke into a bank of microphones.

'Victor Tango, clear for landing, runway one,' said Mike Evans, one of those efficient controllers.

Mike looked up from his control bank, expecting to see the large jumbo lumbering on to the tarmac. He almost died of fright, when he saw Fatty's unenterprising starship bearing vertically down on to the runway.

As he gaped unbelievingly at the hammer and sickle motif and other Russian insignia which decorated this extraordinary craft, Evans barked into his mouthpiece:

'Victor Tango. Overshoot. I say again, overshoot! Obstacle in your path. Please overshoot.'

He was only just in time. Fatty grabbed Robinski and made for a hatch at the back of the ship. When they were safely ensconsed in the plastic bubble-shaped module, Fatty pulled a large red lever on his control panel and the hatch was opened by remote control. They roared off and were soon a speck of yellow perspex in the Bedfordshire sky.

Ground staff swarmed all over the foreign craft. The wailing of sirens mixed with the ringing of bells, as all the airport's many services flew into action. Fire engines, security vehicles and police cars headed for the ship. Soon, people were crawling like ants over the metal superstructure, and soon the human crew would be captured.

Inside the dark bowels of the probe, terrified by the

clattering feet and chattering drills which tried to burst through the thick skin of the machine, Gladys shook so much that her tin body rattled loudly. What would happen to her now? Would she be taken prisoner by the wicked capitalist British? She felt a steel hand on her aluminium shoulder and looked up into the cameras of her very own R-T Far-T.

She stopped shivering – sure that he would save her . . .

CHAPTER EIGHT

Thirty Nine and a half Steps to Scotland

The blob that was Tom turned even greener as Peggy pressed herself closer to Navek for comfort. He oozed between them. Peggy and Navek recoiled as they felt the clammy wobbler next to their skin.

Peggy assumed that her ex-husband must have his back to Navek, for two arm-like things appeared out of his jelly mass and rolled her from him.

'Keep away from each other,' Daleked the splodge.

His attention from this task was diverted, as the radio crackled into life. He flowed over to it, making the sound of an elastoplast being removed from the skin.

'Air control to Major Tom, are you receiving me? Over.'

'Tom here. I am receiving you, Fatman. Where are you?'

'There's been a slight hitch in the Supercede masterplan, Tom. We came down somewhat off course. We landed at Luton Airport. As you know, it should have been Inverness. But, don't worry. We're on our way. Should be with you within the hour and we have, on board, enough serum to keep you humanoid for months. I think we can still salvage the situation. We'll have to eliminate Peggy and Navek, of course, and get ourselves another bird.'

Peggy's eyes rolled in horror at this latest piece of overheard information. She squirmed across the floor until she was back at Navek's side. He comforted her as much as was humanly possible, bound as he was, foot, hand and mouth.

'It shouldn't be too difficult,' the radio staticked on. 'Over and out.'

The green thing, gleeful that his boss was continuing with the master-race plan, jigged around the woodshed with surprising grace for one so sloppy.

Back at Luton, Iva Knockabollockoff was still crouched in her ventilation shaft. The last clatter of footsteps had died away. It must be safe for her to emerge from her hiding place now, she thought. She crawled to the grille at the outlet of the shaft and eased out the gate. She jumped down to the floor and swiftly, but with caution, made her way to Fatty's control room. All was quiet. She encountered no one. At her approach, the doors to the inner sanctum swished open. She was blinded by very bright light.

'They've floodlit it,' she mused perceptibly, 'no doubt, for security reasons.'

Carefully, Iva dropped to the floor and wormed her way to the floor-to-ceiling window. She looked down and saw to her consternation that the starship was surrounded by a circle of heavy-jowled guards. In the brilliance of the floodlights trained carefully upon the vessel, Iva could see that they were all well equipped . . . Their khaki uniforms bulged dangerously with belts of ammunition. They stood like a chorus of Clint Eastwoods, sub-machine guns resting heavily on their hips.

Iva backed away and crouched between the two leather

chairs in the centre of the control deck. Obviously, there was no way out. Even using all her charms, she'd never get past the battalion of marines that were on sentry duty. What could she do? A marine bang was out of the question. And they'd never believe the true story. She had no way of proving that she *was* a double agent. And so top-secret was her cover, that she'd get no help from her superiors in the spy hierarchy. There seemed only one solution . . . Kill herself! After all, she couldn't let her true side down. She flicked open the secret flap at the back of her all-gold pendant. Nestling inside was the little blue pill that would mean instantaneous death. She raised the deadly tablet to her lips, when a brilliant but dangerous scheme flashed into her brain. She would drive the ship out of there!

Trembling, she looked up at the maddening confusion of knobs and switches on the control panel above her head. Where should she start? Confidence returned as she thought of Fatty. If that fat fool could do it, it ought to be a piece of cake for her. On her hands and knees, she hunted around for some form of instructions. He must have had a manual somewhere. She couldn't believe he'd retained the necessary information to fly such a craft. Noticing a crack in the underside of the control panel, she fingered its plastic bottom. All at once, a commodious drawer slid forward. Hidden amongst the *Woman's Owns*, a *Hitch-hiker's Guide To The Galaxy* and several back-issues of *Men Only*, Iva hit upon what she was looking for. The big blue book was inscribed with Fatty's family motto. 'If it moves, fuck it!' was copper-plated in gold leaf upon the hide. Iva flicked through the pages of instructions, but couldn't make head nor tail of the completely blank pages.

'Why would Fatty have a blank manual?' she thought.

Before she could further struggle with this problem, the door of the flight deck flew open. An unearthly clank came from the opening and she spun around in terror. Silhouetted in the blackness of the hole were two puffballs. Iva held her breath. She could hear nothing. Then the rattle of a ray gun shattered the eerie silence. A hot beam of light tore into the plastic beside her. The instruction manual fell to the floor and sizzled and burnt in front of her.

That book had been her last hope . . . Back to the pill. She had it on the tip of her tongue, when the two round balls rolled into the light and her view.

'Gladys,' shrieked Iva. 'Remember me? I stayed for a weekend at the CGB's holiday home . . . with Mr Big.'

R-T Far-T raised his weapon and levelled his sights on Knockabollockoff. Just as he was about to pull the trigger, Gladys, recognising the crouched figure of Iva, gave him an almighty shove. The robot zoomed across the floor and crashed into one of the swivel chairs at Iva's side. The force of the impact up-ended him and he sat down heavily. The chair whizzed around like a spinning top. All Gladys could see was a blur and an occasional flash of two terrified eyes. Glad trundled across the room to Iva.

'Stay where you are,' said Gladys, putting a steely claw on Iva's shoulder. 'If you get up, the guards will see you. We're small enough to get away with it.'

By this time, the chair transporting R-T was slowing to a stop. A very dizzy robot staggered off the carousel and stood swaying giddily beside his alloy ally.

'Why'd you do that?' grumbled R-T.

'I had to save Iva,' replied Gladys. 'She's one of us.'

'Amazing!' said Far-T, 'she looks almost human. What year were you engineered?'

'No, no, no, you silly sausage!' said Gladys. 'She's human. I mean she's on our side. She's with that glorious democratic socialist state of ours. She's one of the big gnomes at the Gremlin.'

'Thank God you recognised me,' said Iva, giving the tin tootsie a big hug. 'I hid in the ventilator shaft when everyone was arrested.'

'But you're not one of the crew,' accused R-T. 'What are you doing on board?'

'Mr Big sent me to watch Fatman. That's all I'm allowed to tell you,' answered Iva, lying through her gold teeth.

'What were you doing when we found you then?' asked the suspicious R-T.

'I was studying Fatman's lift-off manual. But I couldn't understand it – blank pages.'

'Oh, I know all about that,' replied the tin man, 'it was written in invisible ink. Fatso had special glasses in order to read it.'

'It doesn't matter now. Even if we had the glasses. The book's burnt to a cinder.'

A noise like chalk on blackboard, made Gladys and Iva wince. But it was only R-T scratching his head!

'I think I can remember how to fly the ship,' said the robot after some deliberation.

'Eee, ducks, are you sure?' A worried look of metal fatigue creased Gladys' brow.

R-T didn't answer. He ordered the two females to strap themselves into the take-off chairs, but asked Gladys to leave room for him. He rocketed around, twirling this knob and that. Lights flashed incomprehensively all over the huge panel. As the first-stage rocket motors roared into life, R-T squeezed his metal bulk in beside his Glad.

On the ground below them, chaos reigned. At the first rumble from the craft's engines, some of the guards had tried to mount the fuselage, whilst others had flung down their arms in terror and fled. This confusion gave R-T the vital seconds needed for his countdown check-list. The ship slowly began to rise from the tarmac. Little did the escaping trio know, but they almost collided with two jumbos and a passing helicopter. After the amazing lift-off, all personnel in the control tower needed a change of trousers!

R-T executed his delicate task with a surprising skill, and despite the fact that the gooly-grabbing Gladys kept interfering with his lift-off. The only snag was that his lift-off wasn't very large. At fifty feet, the ship levelled off and whizzed sideways. R-T fiddled frantically with knobs and levers in a desperate attempt to get the ship to go upwards. Meanwhile, Gladys was honking into a plastic bag. Iva, sat, strapped to her chair, shut-eyed and limbless. She wished she'd taken her death pill after all!

Using the ship's infra-red scanners, R-T wove between trees and buildings as he continued his fight to gain height. He struggled robotfully to no avail. The best he could hope for was that there were no high hills between Luton and their original destination, Inverness.

With one hand steering between inconveniently planted trees, he hailed his puking partner with the other. Gladys, by now free of her chair, was poking around in the medicine cabinet in a corner. She was looking for a packet of Quells to ward off her air-sickness.

'Where's my sarnies?' intoned the male robot. 'Cucumber on brown,' added the vegetarian automaton in jest.

Gladys dragged the picnic hamper across to the two chairs. Raising the lid, she delved inside and pulled out a shiny bright oilcan.

'Here we are – vegetable oil!' said the delighted Gladys.

She moved over beside him and began tenderly squirting it into all of his joints.

'How's that?' asked Glad, the feast finished.

Before R-T could reply, the engines cut out. The three adventurers froze rigid to their spots, as the rocket ship dropped like a stone. They steeled themselves for the crash.

'Brace, brace,' shouted R-T, as he shoved Gladys' head between her legs in the crash position. He and Iva quickly followed suit and the three bent beings waited . . .

They didn't have to wait long. The triumverate were knocked sideways as the ship slammed into the unyielding ground. The residents of Kinver, thinking it was an earthquake, waited, tremulous, for the earth to swallow them up.

But it didn't. And eventually they crept to their windows, looking for they-knew-not-what. Nothing was to be seen and they soon went back to their slumbers, oblivious to the menace in their midst.

Coming around, the threesome looked at each other in wonder. They were all quite safe.

'Now what?' questioned Iva.

She reached into the map drawer in the control console and took out a chart of Great Britain.

'We're here!' she pointed. 'On Kinver Edge. Outside this big city. It's called Birmingham.'

'And here is Loch McCock.' Iva pointed to the north of the map.

The robots rolled their eyes.

'It's all very well for you,' said R-T, 'you can get there by any means. But Glad and myself are going to be slightly noticeable on Inter-City.'

This geography lesson was broken up by Iva.

'We've got to move fast,' she said. 'Follow me.'

With that, she was out of the door and down the corridor towards the escape hatch. The two robots rollicked after her. She was about to turn the massive metal handle of the hatch, when she heard a scraping noise outside.

'Sssh,' she warned the rattling duo. 'Stand back out of sight. Give me your ray-gun R-T.'

Iva crouched down on the floor and trained her gun on the exit. Even as they watched, the handle twitched and began moving slowly to its unlock position. It stopped and the door shuddered slightly on its hinges. It moved menacingly open. Inch by inch, it lumbered in towards them.

'Freeze!' barked Iva at the shadowy outline of the man who stood on the threshold. 'Drop your weapon!'

A clatter of steel echoed down the corridor as her order was obeyed. The three of them leapt at the shape in the shadows. They scrummed him to the ground. The robots pinned down a leg each, while Iva sat on his head.

The anger the soldier felt at being taken by surprise, vanished as quickly as it had come. He lay still and breathed in the delicate perfume of the strange lady's pussy. He let his limbs go limp. Iva relaxed as he stopped struggling. She moved her crotch across his up-turned face. The soldier stuck out his tongue and licked the silky patch between her legs. The pink probe tried valiantly to force its way through the pink gauze. And it was love at first bite!

The robots, sensing something was amiss, loosed their steely grip on the prisoner. They twirled around, amazed to see the expression on Iva's face. A gold-toothed smile split her face in two. R-T Far-T, worried by this human turn of events, dragged Glad into the shadows. He shielded his lady-love's eyes from the torrid twosome. The khaki-clad person reached up and put his huge hands, either side of Iva's slender frame. He lifted her gently from his face. The supple spy swung her legs backwards. The man smiled up at Iva and lowered her, until her lovely face blossomed like a rose above him. His tongue entered her mouth, pushing her own this way and that. He wrapped his arms around her, pulling her forcefully to him. Her arms snaked around his neck.

In the corner, the robots rattled and fussed worriedly. What were these humans up to? Should they interfere?

R-T decided, though, to hold his electric current and wait!

The humans were now quite bare. Their clothes lay strewn on the corridor floor. They rolled around on their metallic bed in a new-found ecstacy. The man was now on top and forcing his muscular legs between Iva's. She moved to accommodate his bulk. Her bottom squashed into the hard cold floor. She felt his ray gun cock scorch into her stomach. His hot breath played on her neck, as he nibbled her milky white throat. Suddenly, he rolled on his back, pulling her up and over. He tried to place her on his rod but the tool was jerking in all directions. He only succeeded in squashing it; trapping it in her pubic mass. He raised her high. His arm muscles rippled. She shifted her legs until she was sitting square on his chest, with a fleshy barrier either side of his face. He turned to one side and began to lick the virgin flesh above her knee. She threw her head to one side, tossing back her long black hair until it fanned out around her head. She slid her bottom along his frame, only stopping when she came to his chin. He stopped his slurpings and stared her straight between the thighs. She stayed there for about a second and the next thing he knew, she was presenting him with the rounded moons of her bottom. She knelt over his head and, once more, he was treated to her spectacular scenery. A range of delicious pink mountains and valleys hove into view. Looking beyond, down her trim body, he saw the heavenly curvature of her breasts. They swung above his three passion-pieces. They descended. They crushed into him. A hot, hungry mouth devoured first one ball and then the other. She sucked on his seed sack, munching joyously. She rolled one of his balls of sex along her tongue. The pointed tip lapped slowly around this hairy nut. A hand on her neck guided her mouth to his hot shot. Iva took it in, an inch at a time. The intruder was spaced out. It gave Iva one hell of a feeling of power, knowing she was exciting him so much. Her bottom, which was high in the air, was being assaulted. He clawed on it; pulling it downwards. She almost bit an inch off his cock, as his tongue made contact with her pussy. Tremours of passion shook her entire being. He swivelled right around, drawing his body up and let his penis brush against Iva's hot and melting pot. Instead of immediately shafting her, he massaged this area with the glistening tip of his swollen-headed cock. He left her wanting him so badly. The next thing she knew, his tool was teasing her nipple nuts. He poked at the dewey buttons.

'Down,' she begged. 'Go down.'

His cock sloped off in the new direction of her calling clit. He ploughed her furrow. He slammed in and out of her with violent thrusts. Her bruised blossom wilted under his brutal attack. She raised her legs and crossed them around his torso. She gripped tightly, urging him to go faster, plunge deeper. He obeyed and his red-hot poker delved even further into her lovehole.The first tingle of orgasmic lust started deep within the walls of her womb. They spread throughout her body, leaving her breathless and fucked. The cries of their coming echoed around the hollow inside of the starship. R-T Far-T put his fingers in his microphones!

The distant wail of sirens joined their chorus of caterwauling. The soldier, completely captivated by Iva's immense charms, gave all his allegiance to her and took the hairy situation in hand. He quickly introduced himself as Daniel Dere and explained, ironically, that he'd been UFO-spotting when their craft landed.

'We must escape before the troops arrive. Please will you help us?' Iva implored.

'Get yourself and those robots out of the hatch. We'll have to hide – they're almost here! I know this district very well – there's some large caves not far away, in which we can secrete ourselves.'

They struggled into their clothes. Iva and her new friend Dan leapt out of the hatch and on to the ground. They were closely followed by two very worried robots. The bizarre foursome fled the ship and scurried away from the beauty spot. The humans ran and the robots wheeled over the rough ground. They disappeared into a black hole. Search parties sought them all that night. The beams of the searchers' torches even glanced around the interior of their cave and penetrated the blackness of their hole. But they were safely installed upon a narrow ledge – high up in their cavernous cache.

While the robots went into a state of unconsciousness and recharged their batteries, Iva and Dan were able to exchange rings of confidences. In whispers, so that old robot-ears couldn't hear, Iva explained that she was, in fact, a double agent. Further, she was en route to Loch McCock in Scotland and it was imperative that she reach there as soon as possible. The entire universe could depend on it. Awed by the magnitude of this splendid plot, Dan dared to help her.

'We'll have to 39-Step our way to Scotland,' confided Dan. 'But what about the tin persons?'

'I know they're not on our side at present. But they could be useful to us. And later, perhaps we can re-programme them . . .'

'Right,' said Dan, 'our first move must be to get transport out of here. Rouse the robots and tell them we're off.'

Iva prodded R-T and Gladys into action. The four fugitives shuffled out into the gloom. They would have to act quickly; it was already beginning to get light. They trekked over fields and down dales until they came upon a farmstead. The little house was almost completely shrouded in mist. But they could make out the shape of a line of washing in the back yard and the promising silhouette of a large garage.

'You steal some washing Iva and disguise our mechanical friends as well as you can. I'll take a peek in the garage.'

Iva did her best with the *haute couture* available. They soon looked like a couple of stumpy matrons. White blouses and gingham skirts enhanced their lack of curves. Paisley scarves were tied nattily around their large metallic heads.

There was a roar from the garage and a Range Rover came straight through the rotting wooden doors. Dan screeched to a halt in the yard and opened the passenger door and hatchback. This almighty bloody racket disturbed Farmer Giles from his post-coital slumbers. He was at the bedroom window, with his twelve bore in his hand, in a matter of seconds.

'What the fuck's going on? What's all the row about? What are you doing with my Range Rover?'

'Stealing it,' Iva replied saucily, as she leapt into the passenger seat.

The vehicle lurched off, dragging two matrons behind it. The robots were buffetted, bumped and humped all the way down the farm track to the gate on the main road. Dan leapt out, as the robots leapt in. Dere opened the gate, flung himself back behind the wheel, and roared off.

Farmer Giles, his jolly red face purple with anger, dialled for help. Soon the police all over the country had the colour and registration number of the Range Rover and a full description of its weird occupants.

Meanwhile, the fleeing four were sticking to the back-roads. They had just enough sense to realise that all the major routes would be blocked. They continued on, through the Snake Pass, and were making for Sheffield when disaster struck. They had a blow-out and the Range Rover veered all over the road. It ended up upside-down in a ditch. Dan and Iva had clunked and clicked and were consequently unscathed. The robots, however, came off a little the worse for wear. Both had bad dents in their outer metal skins. These weren't very deep and they still functioned normally. The bruised, battered and undamaged foursome clambered out of the wreck and hailed a passing double-decker into Steel City. They alighted outside the Crucible Theatre and made their way to the main shopping precinct. They needed new disguises. It was then that Iva hit upon a brilliant idea. The robots would travel as children! They marched into the Mothercare shop and while Dan chatted up the shop assistants, Iva – with his money – bought enough gear for their needs. They had R-T and Gladys kitted out in romper suits and bonnets in next to no time.

The weird troupe then made their way to the station and with Dan's Barclaycard bought tickets to Inverness. They travelled by local shuttle to Doncaster, changed trains, and were soon installed in a first-class carriage, with their heads resting gently on the white linen headrests. The journey went without a hitch, until the diesel locomotive pulled into Newcastle-upon-Tyne. They peeked out of the window, admiring the excellent view, when they saw a policeman flat-footing towards their carriage. They panicked and threw themselves into the nearest unoccupied lavatory. Iva locked the door. Dan unlocked it again.

'If you leave it unbolted, the chances are they won't look in.'

He'd hardly finished speaking, when they heard the ominous thud, thud, thud of large feet coming down the corridor. The two officers stopped between the two lavatory doors.

'Only one engaged Fred,' said the larger of the two men, 'I'll just give it a knock.'

His fist rapped on the door and the four heard the sound of a bolt being pulled back. The door opened and a worried little face looked out.

'Don't you know there's no peeing when the train's in the station?' asked the reprimanding officer.

The two bluebottles plodded off and up the corridor. The whistle blew and the train chugged out of the station. After ten minutes, the fugitives decided it was safe to come out.

The humans left the babies in the carriage and Dan and Iva treated themselves to a light luncheon in the dining car. It wasn't long before they were pulling into yet another station . . . Edinburgh. Their stop-over was brief and they breathed a sigh of relief when the train pulled out again. But unbeknownst to them, two plain clothes policemen had boarded the train, just as it had begun to move. The sleuths in civvies blended uneasily with the rest of the passengers. They were to carry out a careful search of every inch of the train. It took only minutes for the detectives to get to the runaway's carriage. As they entered the car, Dan recognised them as cops immediately. The two policemen came on along the corridor, approaching the fugitives' compartment. Dan acted quickly. Dashing back to their compartment, he slammed the door, pulled down the blinds and rushed to the window. He opened it wide and a gale of clear Scottish air had the four in its grips.

'Right,' said Dan, as the train thundered on to the Forth Bridge, 'they're searching this carriage. There's nothing else for it, we've got to jump.'

Iva stopped him.

'No, no,' she cried. 'We can use Gladys and R-T. Quick, switch on your magnets and give us a piggy-back out of the window.'

R-T didn't like the sound of this at all. And Gladys wasn't feeling brave either. But they had been programmed to obey and, so, started clambering out of the open window. When the two robots were stuck like glue to the metal carriage, Dan and Iva clambered out after them. They climbed down and clung to their backs while the robots shuffled lower and lower. Eventually, they were almost on top of the wheels. When they reached this point, the robots side-stepped and slid right under the carriage. Their human piggy-backs clung on for all they were worth as the track, not more than a foot away, whistled past their ears.

Inside, the two policemen had burst into the shuttered compartment, guns at the ready. They'd been greeted by a gust of wind.

'They've jumped!' said one to the other, as he pulled on the communication cord.

The huge iron maiden screeched in protest at this abrupt treatment. The wheels locked, showering the fugitives with sparks. As the train slowed to a walking pace, the eager cops leapt to the ground. They ran up and down the track, looking on both sides of the train. But they could see nothing.

'They must have jumped before we reached the bridge,' said one cop to the driver. 'They can't have got far. We'll go back and look for them. You carry on.'

CHAPTER NINE

A Gilbertian Situation

The door swung open. A syringe appeared. On the end of it was a breathless Fatman. And on the end of him, an even more breathless Robinski.

'Another monster!' whispered Peggy, snuggling into Navek's manly chest.

'No. It's only Fatman, the most venomous man in the galaxy,' breathed Navek.

The green slime, dressed in Tom's green shirt and levis, fawned across the room and tried to gather itself up into some sort of greeting.

An adenoidal voice broke from the jelly: 'Welcome Fatman. And not a moment too soon.'

'Sorry about the slight delay,' spake the corpulent one. 'Overshot the loch. My module looks a little rough. It's smashed into the rocks at the other end of the island. But never mind that; give me an arm and I'll give you your shot.'

The green blob pushed out an amoeboid tentacle.

A glint of steel caught the light from the broken window above and then disappeared into the green jelloid lump. Having administered the dose, Fatman stepped back to watch the transformation. It was almost immediate.

Robinski, Navek and Peggy were goggle-eyed at the ghoul. It wobbled and shook and, suddenly, a human head popped out of the floppiness. This was soon followed by two arms, two legs and a torso. With a few last remaining dribbles of green running down his face, Tom stood before them.

'Now that you're back in your human shape, we must lose no time in finding another female specimen to be your mate. We must dispose of these inconveniences,' he pointed sinisterly at Navek and Peg, 'as quickly as possible.'

Tom swung his bulk around slowly and surveyed his pretty one-time wife.

'Do we have to go to those lengths?' he said with a flash of regret in his eyes.

He crossed over to Peglet and bent down, cupping her face in a hand.

'She's such a pretty little thing. It's a shame to waste all that succulent flesh. Those long, strong legs . . . those amazing breasts . . . rock-hard nipples . . . sex-sucking lips . . .'

Tom seemed to be turning quite human.

Peggy, who had shuddered at the first feel of this felon, was almost sick with fear at the way he was going on.

'Can I give her one for old time's sake?' the eager Tom asked Fatman, making to unzip his jeans.

Peggy looked up in terror and she saw the familiar bulge of his banana getting bigger.

'Please . . . no,' she shrilled, and it was her turn to stiffen – with fright!

'There's no time for oats,' chastised Fatman. 'We'll have porridge instead. Now, off you trot Robinski and make three bowls of the steaming stuff. And make sure mine has plenty of brown sugar and cream. I know you're no Cradock, but you sure have a lovely fanny! We're going to sort out the best way of disposing with this pair. Your delicate ears shouldn't ever have to hear such dastardly details.'

Robinski scurried out of the shed with an extreme look of surprise on her face. He'd never shown such concern before . . .

The thought of porridge made Navek and Peggy realise they'd been imprisoned – lying in this draughty shed – for the past two days. And with nothing to eat at all. They were starving . . . ravenous.

'What about us?' wailed Peggy. 'Please, give us something to eat.'

'You don't need anything to eat. You won't be hungry long. You'll be dead soon,' comforted the corpulent one.

'You dirty bastard!' spat Navek through his gag.

Robinski moved happily around the kitchen, laying the table, and setting out three monster bowls of Scottish oats. When everything was ready, she ran off down the garden path to call the man and monster to table. Two pairs of eyes watched her leave and made a dash for the food. This four were starving too . . .

By the time the terrible trio trooped into the kitchen, two of the porridge bowls were licked clean and the other had the marks of a strange-footed bird in the goo that remained.

'Who's been eating my porridge?' said Fatman, pouncing on his bowl.

'Don't be so silly,' snapped Robinski. 'Stop messing about. I don't like this. Something really strange is going on here. Look at the marks in this bowl. They weren't made by any human hand.'

The two earthlings looked suspiciously towards Tom. He caught their questioning gaze.

'I was in the shed with you,' he said. 'I haven't anything to do with this. Anyway, we're all friends. On the same side. I wouldn't double-cross you!'

Fatman looked reassured. He wouldn't have done, however, had he seen what was going on outside. Iva and Dan had instructed R-T and Gladys to stand guard at the garden gate. Iva didn't want them to see what she and her soldier were up to. After all, they would rush to Fatman's aid, and ruin their plans. Stealthily, she and Dan crept around the house. Iva positioned herself outside the back door, while Dan let himself in by the front and crept across the hall to the kitchen. They'd synchronised their watches and, at the appointed second, kicked the doors in and flung themselves into the fray.

'Reach,' they shouted in unison, brandishing their ray guns at the bandits.

Fatman's fat hand lunged for his holster. But Dan was too quick for him and squeezed his trigger. The stunned Fatman fell to the floor.

Robinski was stunned too. Not by a ray gun, but by the sight of Iva Knockabollockoff, her lesbian legover. With mixed emotions, she asked:

'Who are you?'

Before Iva could answer, Fatman came to. His beady eyes fixed on Iva. She smiled victoriously at the creep on the floor. A glint of gold gnashers and recognition blinded the poor sod.

'It's Mr Big's whore,' he shouted to Robinski. 'She was at the ball – don't you remember?'

'Well, it was so dark there, I could hardly see anything,' said Robinski, somewhat flustered. She silently prayed that Iva would not disclose their intimate lesbian act to Fatman. If she did, all would be up. Visions of salt mines filled her with terror.

'Oh, yes it's her all right,' continued Fatman, 'You traitor,' he screeched. 'You treacherous vassal.'

'Enough of that you fat fool. Talk about the pot calling the kettle black. We know all about your proposed super-race. And as for you . . . ' she stared hard at Tom, 'you're nothing but a green blob.'

Dan, all this time, had become increasingly confused.

'And what have you done with my boss Navek?'

None of the three answered.

'You'll tell me sooner or later,' continued Iva, approaching Fatman.

She sauntered up to the large person, smiled, swung a leg and gave him a vicious blow in the balls. He doubled over, writhing in agony. Iva didn't have to ask a second time. The gibbering cowardly mess on the floor wheezed the answer to her question.

'He's in the garden shed.'

'Lead the way, fat guts,' said Iva, driving the barrel of her raygun between his buttocks.

The blubber shambled to its feet and led the way out of the kitchen door and up the garden path . . . again! Dan brought up Iva's rear and soon the quintet reached the bolted door of the lean-to. Iva viciously snatched the key from Tom's neck and almost severed his head from his body.

'You cover them Dan, while I unlock the door.'

Her agile fingers played with the padlock; the clasp broke open and the door swung back. She leapt inside and bounded straight to Navek's side. She unravelled him from his constricting bonds. He leapt up and freed Peg.

'So you're the perfect specimen,' said Iva, looking the dishevelled Peg up and down with disdain.

'Well done,' said Navek, 'you'll get the Martian Cross for this.'

The miscreants found themselves hog-tied and gagged on the dirty floor of the cold dark cellar below the house. All except Tom. Navek, with great foresight, had forced Tom's large body into an empty beer barrel and had hammered down the lid. In a few hours time, he'd revert to his green and jelloid state. Navek was taking no chances. He'd never ooze out of this tight drum.

With the baddies safely out of the way, the four now had time to decide what to do. But their sexual and nutritional needs had to be appeased first. As the quartet made their way to the kitchen to raid the larder and stuff themselves silly, Peg glanced at her tub of indoor plants. The last time she'd seen those, they'd been trying to strangle her. The effects of the serum had obviously worn off and the plants had shrunk back to their normal size.

Over a simple repast, they talked. All was explained to Dan, who listened open-mouthed to the enormity of Fatman's audacity and atrocities. They decided that there was little more they could do that day. They would wait until the morrow and then take their captives to Navek's headquarters in the sky.

This night was theirs . . .

Peggy and Navek lay side by side in the bountiful bosom of the floral four-poster, while they exchanged whispers. Next door, however, in the spare room, Dan and Iva mouth-organed noisily. Peg and Navek could hear the slurp, slurp of sex-suckings through the thin partition between boudoirs. They *had* intended to curl up together and drift into a much-needed sleep. But the carnal concerto from next door raised Navek's flagpole. Peggy, too, found herself aroused by the others. She reached down, knowing she would encounter an engorged cock. She wasn't wrong! Her fingers fastened around its tumescence. Her fiery touch made that age-old awe-full tingle tear through his tool. It had been so long since he'd shot his love-load. The thought of penetrating her glory hole moved him urgently. He rolled on top of her. His seed-sower sought out her pot of gold at the end of her sexual rainbow. Her pussy lips parted, as he nudged his pink submarine up her yellow prick road. Within seconds Navek came, leaving Peggy frustrated by his burst of premature ejaculation. Soon, his pride and joy slunk out, leaving Peg wide-legged and come-less.

'I'm so sorry, my beloved Peg. I couldn't help myself. After the trials and tribulations in the shed, I needed you more than anything.'

'That's all right my dearest. Don't worry. It's wonderful

for a woman to feel herself needed so much by the man she loves. I love it when you just take me and fuck me. It doesn't matter if I don't come. You make me feel the most fragile, most feminine woman in the world.'

These tender words went like a red rag to his balls. They thumped with a new load of lust liquid. He turned her on her side and guided his longboat between her thighs. She squeezed her legs together and moved her buttocks slowly backwards and forwards. The sodden sex-slug slowly slipped around the surrogate slit of her thighs. The bent front of his cock rubbed softly against her clit, activating the lips of her sex-bomb. This nuclear charge worked on his semi-flaccid tool and it began its ascent. His hand moved down and pressed against her merry mound. Cries of wanton lust broke from her lips. Peggy wriggled and jiggled and squiggled until the slippery snake plunged inside her.

The noises of their coming – in unison this time – could be heard quite plainly next door, where Dan had his head buried in Iva's crotch. His tongue toiled furiously on her pink pleasure button. When Navek's groans reached his ears, Dan pushed his tongue further and further and higher and higher into Iva's tender trap. As Navek boomed 'I'm coming,' it brought back to Iva the past moments of lust she'd shared with the super-spy. In her mind's eye, she saw his marvellous manhood in all its pulsating glory. As Dan's tongue tore into her lubricating love-box, she relived the sensation of Navek's wide wonder parting her pussy waves and sliding into her ocean of sex.

'Fuck me, fuck me, Dan,' she cried out, as she grabbed a handful of his hair and pulled his head out and his cock in. It shot into her like a blow torch through solder. She melted away in the hot flames of his desire. She was barely conscious; steeped in a sexual haze. She hardly noticed as he rolled over and took her forcibly with him. She ended up on top.

His cock was still firmly embedded in her soft marshmallow centre. His hands clawed at her buttocks, as he helped her to fuck him. Her bum bobbed up and down, as his lubricating length lunged in and out. With an extra thrust, Dan threw his ride-a-cock-horsewoman into the air. He caught her neatly on the end of his pole; turned her over and pushed her deep into the mattress. He banged her hard, until his sex piston unloaded its twin ball-barrels deep within her. As he ended his highway to heaven, she began her pathway to paradise. He held on to her, until her violent shudders of passion subsided.

A flash of white light and a thundering roar made Dan jump to the window. In the next room, Navek was at his dormer too. The two men watched, horror-struck, as a space module swept dangerously past the overhanging eaves of thatch. Then, it headed off into the black hole that was sky.

The four dressed hurriedly, throwing on clothes as they bounded down the stairs. They rushed straight to the cellar and confirmed their worst suspicions. The door gaped open. The birds had flown. The module they'd seen flying past must have been theirs.

'I thought Fatman said he'd damaged his module when he landed . . .' said Navek, confused.

'Where did he say the crash happened?' asked Dan.

'On the other side of the island.'

'Let's go!' said Iva decisively.

Taking torches from the kitchen drawer, they headed for the scene of the crash landing. Within five minutes, they were drawing close to the rocks on the other side of the island. Navek, who was leading the way, suddenly motioned them to get down and be quiet.

'What is it?' hissed Peggy in Navek's ear. She was crouching silently beside him.

'Didn't you hear anything? There it is again.'

The four could plainly hear low eerie moans and the rattle of metal on metal. The strange sounds came from the rocks directly in front of them. They edged slowly closer.

Navek parted the leaves of the bush they were hiding behind and there, on the ground, were two dark round humps. The noises were coming from them. Silently, Navek motioned the three to circle around the shapes. But keeping well hidden by the bushes.

'We'll take them by surprise,' he whispered.

Armed to the hilt with Fatty's weapons, the four crept in a circle around the odd shapes. On a signal from Navek, they leapt from the undergrowth and shone their torches on the unidentified groaning objects.

R-T Far-T and Gladys, now a pile of twisted metal, looked up pathetically. They tried to shield their optics from the glare of the torches.

'It's all right Navek – it's our friendly robots.'

Iva dashed to their side and began untangling their entwined limbs, saying 'there, there' a lot.

'Give me a hand here,' she barked. 'We must get them back to the croft.'

They took a metal bundle each between two and set off apace across the heather. Reaching the house, they lay the aluminium bundles out on the sofa. While Iva and Peggy dashed about with lint and Dettol, Navek gently questioned them.

'What happened?' he soothed.

R-T began the tale of woe:

'We'd been guarding the front gate like Miss Knockabollockoff had told us to, when we heard this kerfuffle coming from the depths of the house. We'd seen the lights go off upstairs and knew, therefore, that you were all safely tucked up in bed. So, we felt it our duty to investigate. We crept down to the cellar door and looked through the porthole window. We were just in time to see – with our infrared vision – the last globules of some sort of jelly flowing out of the bunghole in a barrel. And then we saw our master Fatman.'

'Good grief,' exclaimed Navek, 'the jelloid alien must have

mustered all its strength and pushed out the cork. I wouldn't have thought he'd have been able to ooze through that hole.'

'But he did, but he did,' said R-T excitedly, his main circuits showing definite signs of strain.

'Calm yourself,' said Navek, 'or you'll blow a fuse.'

'I couldn't understand why my boss was locked up. I only knew I had to help him. I opened the door and pushed Gladys down the steps. Then followed on behind her. I released the two tied prisoners and we followed Fatman, who led us straight to his damaged module. There, he instructed Gladys and myself to repair the crumpled vehicle. It took us four hours of fussing to get it space-worthy. Once it was operational, Fatman, Robinski and the alien jumped in. We were about to follow, when they closed the hatch door on us. It broke my arm, broke Glad's leg and broke my electronic heart. Moi, who'd faithfully served that man for so long! How could he discard me like an old tin can?'

Eight eyes moistened at this pathetic saga . . .

R-T carried on, anger replacing his chagrin:

'And what really got me, was the way they manhandled my poor Gladys. She's a real lady, not used to all this rough stuff. She was living a sheltered life in a holiday camp before I met her. It makes my oil boil.'

As if to illustrate this point, vast quantities of steam poured out of his microphonic ears. His outer casing began to tremble.

'Careful, dear,' said Gladys, 'remember your high oil pressure. You'll have another seizure in a minute.'

Still trembling with technological emotion, R-T began a strange soliloquy:

'That Fatman has destroyed my faith in the red Russian way of life. We don't want to return to that drab grey country. We're going to defect. We'd like to stay here at Loch McCock. I can tend the gardens and Gladys can do the housekeeping. She's a good little scrubber and I've got green claws! We can turn the cellar into our quarters. Will that be all right?'

Peggy, being the only regular inhabitant of the island, replied: 'Of course, I'd be delighted to have you. Finding good human help these days is so difficult!'

'Thank you, ma'am,' said Gladys, rattling up and down in excitement at this capitalist turn of events.

The convalescent couple trundled happily off down the garden path – away to their new basement home. The moon shone brightly, and glinted on their dented heads, as their politics repositioned in their electrodes – swinging sharply from red to blue.

CHAPTER TEN

Superknob meets his match

The famous four gasped in terror as everything cut off. The lights flickered and flashed and then petered out.

At the control panel of Tom's hijacked space ship, Navek, sweating profusely, battled manfully with the equipment. Across from the central steering unit, Dan Dere was trying to kick some life into the sophisticated communications equipment.

All functions of the space craft had ceased. And yet they all had a curious feeling of buoyancy. In front of them was a gigantic crimson funnel of light. They'd never encountered anything like it before.

'Dan,' barked Captain Navek, 'what was our position when we lost power?'

'We were following Fatman as we entered the Bermuda Triangle,' Dan replied.

'How the hell are we maintaining height with no power? It's as if the light is lifting us.'

The crimson glow wrapped itself around them. They were sucked into the centre of the bleeding vortex. The light licked like flames around the craft, as if to consume them. They were being held steady by the force of the carmine whirlpool. The heavy ship floated, weightless, buoyed up by this strange vermilion power.

Peggy, frozen to the spot, glanced around at the ruddy glow which the intense light was casting on the faces of the crew. Navek and Dan had given up their struggle to regain control of the craft. They gazed in wonder at this intergalactic firework display. The phenomenon mesmerised them. They were powerless. A small cry broke from Peggy as she brushed against the fuselage.

'What's wrong?' questioned Navek.

'The walls are getting hot. We're going to fry. We'll be cooked alive.'

Dan reached out and touched the inner skin of the ship.

'She's right, Navek,' he said, pulling his hand quickly away. 'The fuselage is getting very hot.'

'OK,' said the quick-witted Nav, 'get into the padded chairs and strap yourselves in.'

'No. I won't,' said Peggy and she started to scream hysterically. The events of the last few days were beginning to catch up with her.

Navek strode across to her, slapped her hard on the cheek and pushed her down in the nearest chair.

'Stay there, you little fool. It's your only chance to come out of this alive.'

Peggy sat whimpering quietly in her chair.

Immediately they were all secure, the ship began to slowly rotate. It was almost as if something, somewhere had been watching them. The ship gathered momentum. It was soon spinning like a top. The space travellers felt no sensation of dizziness or nausea – just a feeling of ascent. It was as though they were being pulled sharply upwards by a hugely powerful unknown force. It was taking them higher and higher. Through the portholes, they could see the core of the molten maelstrom turning gold. As their spiral continued, the centre changed colour constantly. They flashed up into the heart of colour and the control deck was ringed by a constantly changing halo of light. The irridescence captivated them. It shed lustre throughout the entire ship.

Watching in awe, they noticed a tiny pinprick of bright white light appear in the centre of the kaleidoscopic cyclone. The prick grew in brightness and dimension. It would consume them. The end was nigh. This was the silent thought of the souls on board that starship.

They were getting closer and closer to the source of the bright white light. They shielded their eyes from the intense incandescent glow. The craft began to shudder as it neared the brilliant orb. There was a loud report and they shot like popping corn through the colour warp. They were rocketed out into a sky of brilliant blue. At its outermost edges, they could make out the familiar black of deep outer space. In the very centre of their line of vision, their eyes were arrested by a planet that was the earth's twin. They could see the familiar land masses and oceans of their mother planet.

The craft's spinning had ceased and Navek was the first to unbuckle himself from his chair. As the others got to their feet, Navek retook his place at the central control panel. The malfunctioning equipment was once more operative. Navek, eager to retake the helm of his ship applied himself to his task. He moved this control and that, in a vain attempt to regain control of the steering.

'I can't change course,' he cried out desperately. 'We are locked firmly on to a collision trajectory with that planet. Dan, can you raise anything?'

Dan, at the radio, smiled.

'Nothing on this machinery,' he answered, 'but my own rocket could blast off with a little help from my friend!'

'There's no need to be so damned droll,' snapped Navek. 'This is a serious situation. We've no idea what life lurks on this strange world. Nor if the atmosphere will support us. Or indeed if it's inhabited. And by what and by whom.'

'Maybe it's full of jolly green jelly babies,' quipped Iva.

Peggy shivered.

'Not more of those,' she pleaded.

'We'll soon find out,' said Navek. 'We've got about five and a half minutes to touch-down. There's nothing we can do. We can't even choose where we land. The only good thing about this mess is that whoever or whatever is guiding us down to this strange new world must be somewhat friendly. A hostile manipulator could easily have blasted us to smithereens before now.'

As if in raucous answer to this private question, Fatman beamed himself into their midst. The space travellers were aghast at the rotund apparition.

'Fuck, not you again,' said Navek irreverantly. 'Get him.'

Dan, Peg and Iva moved for their weapons. They aimed carefully and fired. Four streams of white deadly light rebounded off four invisible force fields. The friends tried to move, only to discover that they were hemmed in on all sides. Fatman had them, once more, in his podgy clutches.

With a cackle of evil laughter, he addressed them. 'It is pointless to struggle,' said the maniac, his mad eyes burning through their skulls.

'You were unwise enough to come after me, now you'll pay for learning the secret of the Bermuda Triangle. It has always been one of the greatest mysteries of mankind. I will tell you its secret, before I turn you into automatons at my beck and call.'

Fatman's eyes misted as he remembered the first time his ship had accidentally got sucked into the vermilion vortex.

He'd been on a routine reconnoitre for the Russians, boldly searching out planets for the brothel chain. He had been en route from Puerto Rico to Bermuda when, traversing the notorious three-sided area, his ship had been drawn into the spectacular whirlwind. He'd thought all was lost. He'd prepared for death. But when he'd been shot through the end of the vortex and had landed on this paradise of a planet, he'd realised that he'd cracked the secret of the black Bermudan magic box.

'As you lot found out, once inside this peculiar phenomenon, your ship is taken over by outside forces. You can't steer off course. You are compelled to land on this planet. For me, this was an exceedingly happy accident. This hospitable Planet of Eden was exactly what I'd been looking for to start my super-race of super-beings.'

So engrossed was Navek by this startling revelation from Fatman, that he forgot his precarious position and ventured a question.

'So, are all the people from the boats and planes that disappeared without trace, while navigating the Bermuda Triangle, on this planet?'

'I'm afraid not,' answered Fatman. 'You won't get any help from those quarters. The vortex extends right down to sea level and can home in on any vessel or aircraft. Unfortunately, all of the ships and planes that were attracted by the maelstrom were not designed to stand its supernatural force. Once in its grip, they disintegrated. Spaceships, though, can withstand those forces. And mine was the first such vehicle to encounter the vortex.

'You've really sealed your fates this time, you interfering bunch of busy-bodies. I'm thrilled you followed me. It will save me a great deal of time. Now, once we land, you men will be made half robot/half man and slave to your master . . . ME. And you women will be mates for my latest invention. I shall have my master race after all!'

With those words, he beamed off. The four comrades in space stood in silence, agog at what they'd heard.

'We're sunk this time,' wailed Peg despondently. 'I wish I'd stayed in Scotland.'

'I told you it could be dangerous,' said Navek, 'but you wouldn't have it. You insisted on coming. But don't worry. The fat man's a fool. There's bound to be some way we can throw a spanner in his evil works.'

The others stayed silent, battling with their inner fears. The ship touched down on Fatty's paradise. All four made their way to the exit hatch. They stood in front of the steel doors and watched, horrified, as they opened to reveal a gaggle of gargantuan robots. Their transparent heads looked like chrome-tipped electric light bulbs. Within the plastic crania, they spied a profusion of wires, diodes, transistors and silicon chips. The extra-terrestrial beings stood seven feet tall. Their lumbering bodies were transparent too and packed with a mass of sophisticated electronic equipment. Even the arms and legs bristled with bionics.

The mechanical monsters disarmed the prisoners and frog-marched them to Fat Guts. Fatty's lair resembled a modern Crystal Palace; a sophisticated, up-to-the-minute house of glass. They entered the main doors through a Gothic arch of glass and were forced along a corridor of crystal. At the end was an ornately-engraved mirror door. They passed through the looking glass and into the mad hatter's wonderland. There sat Fatso, resplendent upon his glass swivel chair. Robinski was at his side. His back was to them and they could see his bullet head on the massive shoulders beneath. With not a word, he swivelled to face them. His massive thighs strained against the material of his flying suit.

'Now you will all see my creation. I've had my scientists working around the clock to perfect it. I had so much trouble with my alien superstud – what with the fuss over the serum and the problem with his sperm not being potent – that I decided to construct my own male mate. He's ready now – he's perfect. And he takes orders only from me. He's completely servile and has a never-ending supply of fertile sperm. I have no further use for Tom. He will be turned into half man/half robot, just like you two. But before you're made my slaves, I've got a treat in store for you. You can witness your womenfolk being penetrated by my supercock.'

'You filthy swine,' shouted Navek, moving in for the kill. Dan was right behind him. But four perspex arms restrained them. They were forced back and held impotent.

'Now my dear,' said the greasy pig to Peggy. 'As you were my first choice for Mother Earth, you can have the pleasure of the first fuck. Guards.'

Seconds later, Peggy found herself strapped to a weird contrivance in the centre of the room. It was rather like a dentist's chair, except her feet were held by leather restraints which forced her legs up and out. She'd been stripped of her clothing and made to sit bolt upright. Fatman didn't want her to miss anything.

'Come in Superknob!' commanded Fatman.

The being appeared through the door. Peggy shrieked as it stood waiting for Fatman's orders. The mechanical stud – Fatty's grand opus – was the most perfect facsimile of a man. His flesh resembled flesh, his hair resembled hair. An onlooker couldn't have known that he was completely manufactured from robot-made fibre. The only problem was that there was a clit where his cock should have been. Peggy heaved a huge sigh of relief. Perhaps Navek *was* right and Fatty had screwed it up yet again. Her feeling of well-being didn't last for long, though . . .

'Get it up, Superknob,' barked Fatman.

A click, whirr and a whine came from the groin of the being. The humans gasped as an enormous phallus grew from between the robot's thighs. The cock grew and grew like Jack's proverbial beanstalk. It didn't stop until it was seventeen inches long and exceedingly thick in its girth. The cock was as stiff as a broom handle and as proud as a peacock.

Fatman barked another command and Superknob strode purposefully towards Peg's pussy. He was on the point of penetrating the terrified girl, when the door burst open and all hell broke loose.

The rat-a-tat tat of Tom's ray machine gun fused the perspex people who were guarding the three humans. Freed, the trio dashed to Peg's assistance. She had fainted at the approach of Wonder Weapon and had not yet come to. They snatched her from the cock's clutches, but froze in their tracks as Fatman levelled his gun at them.

'Not so fast,' said the hopping mad fat one.

'You dirty rat,' screamed Tom. 'Going to make me a slave, are you? You double-crossing bastard. Take this.'

A deadly ray spat from his gun. It fractured the wall behind Fatty's chair.

'Drop your weapon, you're covered. My kinsman is behind you.'

'I'm not falling for that old trick,' cried Fatman.

Behind him, the green lump of jelly reached out a tentacle and placed a soggy paw on Fatty's shoulder. He jumped around in fright and found himself facing Tom's reinforcement.

'You thought I was joking didn't you Fatman?' said Tom. 'But I had a feeling you'd try and trick me. So I cloned myself last night, just in case. I'm going to take you and your terrible invention to my planet. You'll be a great attraction in our local zoo!'

All this time, Superknob, thwarted in mid-thrust, had been trying to cock a leg over Robinski. He'd been rattling around the room in hot and lustful pursuit of her.

Tom ordered Fatman to turn off his creation. The latter stalked across the room and attempted to throw the on/off switch at the back. At the peak of his programme, however, Superknob was now desperate for a fuck. He flung a leg over Fatman's shoulders, his mammoth knob drilling into the fat person's chest. Just as the pneumatic cock was about to drill into Fatty, he managed to get an arm around to the robot's control. Superknob froze in mid-mount.

The humans had watched this unearthly tableau unfold with great amazement. Now that Tom had dealt with the baddies, it was likely he'd turn to the goodies. What was to be their fate?

In answer to their silent query, Tom turned his attention on them. His eyes narrowed as he pondered the four earthlings. When his glance got to Peg, the green orbs widened and the features softened. The girl felt an old familiar flutter under her breast-bone, as she remembered his sexual prowess. Now he was no longer green, she felt it hard to think of him in any other way except that of her loving husband.

Faltering, she phrased a question: 'Whatever did happen to my real husband? Is he still alive somewhere?'

'And what of Violet?' added Navek.

Peggy desperately hoped that Tom would tell her that *he* was her husband and that there'd been some terrible mistake. But his reply did little to comfort her.

'I'm afraid the evil fat slob found it necessary to eliminate him. It was quite painless. Regretably Violet had to be disposed of also.'

Peg's lips trembled and a large solitary tear rolled down her cheek.

'What's to become of us?' she wailed.

Tom studied the girl. She stood there, childlike and very appealing. He'd dosed himself with so much serum that he was beginning to feel truly human. In fact, he felt something he'd never felt before; a wave of pity for this waif in space. Although she was a little the worse for wear, she still looked exceedingly appetising. Her mass of blonde hair hung in untidy curls over her shoulders. All traces of make-up had long-since disappeared. And she had tiny blue shadows under her eyes. This, however, enhanced her natural beauty. He'd never seen her look so lovely.

His tone became almost benign as he answered Peg's question:

'Fortunately for you, I haven't enough room in my space-ship for four more passengers. I'm going to lock you up and leave you here.'

While his friend, the green blob, marched the villains of this piece off to the spaceship in preparation for blast-off to Spermola, Tom escorted the four, Nav, Peg, Iva and Dan out of Fatty's lair and locked them in separate quarters.

Navek sat down on the bed in his own cell and thought how very strange it was of Tom to leave them here. And especially to use the feeble excuse that there was no room in the spaceship. Something was wrong . . .

He was right. Next door, in Peggy's cabin, Tom was pulling off her clothes. She had no fight left in her; she didn't want to be taken by this strange being, and yet she felt excited. He was after all an exact replica of her husband. And his green and jelloid shape seemed a million light years away. As he touched her tenderly on the cheek, she found it difficult to imagine him in any other form than the present one. She certainly didn't find him repulsive. But, nevertheless, she was glad she was still on the pill and that there'd be no green jelly babies for her!

She closed her eyes and gave herself up to the sweet sensation of his strokings. He pushed her back against the wall and ran his thumb over her left nipple. His hand moved on, seeking out places more intimate. He ran his fingers through her tousled tangle of curls and one unruly digit found its way through her lower lips. Her legs buckled under her. He scooped her into his arms and laid her gently on the bed. Eyes still closed, she lay there waiting for the worst . . . or would it be the best. Confused, she heard the sound of his zip descending. Then, his weight was on her. And he was in her. She had no more time to think as pleasure numbed her brain.

CHAPTER ELEVEN

Captain's Log

Captain's Log.
Starship: Space Probe II of the Milky Way fleet.
Stardate: Unknown.
Crew: Captain Navek; First Mate Miss Peggy; First Officer Daniel Dere; Second Mate: Ms Knockabollockoff.
Position: Earth-bound.
Destination: Loch McCock.
Captain Navek reporting, continuing my log where I left off:

'Have escaped from Fatty's paradise, the Planet of Eden. Indeed, it seems that Major Tom had wanted us to get away. Peggy had told me, with some little embarrassment, of her final fuck with Tom. She explained to me how difficult she had found it to resist the man in his human form. After he'd left her, she had been delighted to find that he'd left the door open. Immediately, she'd released all of us. Iva and Dan had nothing to report other than that they had been locked up and left to themselves. For myself, all I remember after being taken into my cell was sitting on the bed. And then darkness enveloped me. It was Peggy who roused me. She'd found me shirtless, lying on the floor.

'As far as I could tell, all members of the crew, including myself, were physically and mentally fit after our ordeal.

'We left as quickly as we could and made our way to the spaceship. There was no other sign of life – human or otherwise. We were amazed but very grateful to find our ship refuelled, recharged and ready to go. Some force was with us! We climbed aboard and quickly took up our lift-off positions. We punched up on the computer the reverse trajectory to our inward flight. But the electronic help replied that the course was set. There was only one way out of there – the way we'd come in – through the swirling coloured vortex into the atmosphere high above the Bermuda Triangle.

'We took off three hours ago. Now, far ahead of us we can see the first arc of colour that will soon suck us into its irresistible core. I will place this log in the special black-space-box, in case we don't come out of this . . .

'Captain Navek signing off. Kissy, kissy!'

CHAPTER TWELVE

Beauty and the Beast

Loch McCock. Peggy's senses were thrilled to their very roots by the sight of her beloved homestead nestling in the briny bosoms of the loch. The gentle slopes were purple-hued. There was a nip of frost in the air, and the smell of woodsmoke and damp autumn leaves. The small dinghy ran aground on the small worn pebbles of the beach. Navek splashed into the icy water and helped Peggy from the boat. She missed her footing, falling knee-deep in the glacial waters. But nothing could dent her delight at being safely home with her beloved man. The nightmare (that was this book!) was left far behind; a dark and distant dream. She was back in Scotland and intended to keep her feet firmly planted on this earth's rich soil. No more galaxy gallivanting for this ex-Galactic Girl. Navek had promised never to venture into outer space again. They were going to live on the land, be self-sufficient; growing enough to live on and raise a huge family.

With Navek's strong arm about her frail slender body, she pushed forward, urgent to cross over the threshold of home. The weak winter sun was saying good-night. Nature had finished weaving her thick carpet of fire-coloured leaves.

Spiky bare trees made a prickly pattern against the azure sky. Although it was not yet dark, a wafer-thin crack of a crescent moon hung high in the heavens. Peggy looked up at the star-studded ceiling above. She shivered. The cold clear beauty fascinated her, but she felt no compulsion to get any closer. A star should stay in the sky; a human, on earth; and never the twain should meet.

'God, it's good to be home,' cried Peggy, as she and Navek meandered along the banks of the loch.

'It's fantastic,' replied Navek, as he pulled Peggy towards him.

His lips brushed hers in the lightest embrace. She breathed deeply, inhaling the evening air.

'There's something about Scotland,' she said, 'I feel marvellous already. It's this air, it's like pure oxygen to my lungs. A few deep breaths calm me and restore my vitality. I almost feel human again,' she added with a weak smile.

'I'll make it all up to you,' soothed Navek, planting a sweet kiss on her brow. 'You never need worry again. I'll look after you.'

They walked on, arm-in-arm, and were soon at the top of the gentle slope that lead to the croft. The lovers stopped and turned back to enjoy the view. The light was fading fast now but this only enhanced the beauty and silence of the evening. Away, in the distance across the loch, the dark dramatic outline of the hills was splashed across the skyline – bold black brush-strokes across canvas. Above the jagged silhouette of the mountains, the stars were brightly polished gems ready for setting in a platinum crown. The lights of the small hamlet at the foot of the range of hills, came on one-by-one, and danced merrily on the black ripples of loch water. Doors slammed to, 'good-nights' echoed on the air and a hush descended upon the land.

The cuddling lovers wrapped their arms tighter around each other and walked the last few steps to their home. They were approaching the clearing at the front of the house.

Navek held back a needle-covered bough and Peggy stepped out from the shrubbery and into the open. She gasped as she got her first close view of her home. The front door was wide open and moths fluttered around it, hypnotised by the bright shaft of electric light which flooded out on to the garden path.

R-T Far-T and Gladys, their metalwork polished to perfection, stood outside the porch. Drawing closer, the lovers could see the welcome mat. The W had slipped a little – it was Gladys' first attempt at weaving. Nevertheless, it delighted the returning couple. Peggy dropped a kiss on each shiny tin dome.

'How lovely to see you. You both look so well,' said Peggy.

'And very smart,' added Navek.

'We went to the local panelbeaters and had all our dents knocked out,' replied R-T proudly. 'It was very painful but worth it. We were beginning to look a bit the worse for wear, what with the Range Rover crash and Fatman's rude blast-off.'

'You've seen the last of his fat backside,' comforted Navek.

Gladys, thrilled to her wheels, shouted: 'Welcome ma'am, welcome sir,' and tried to execute a curtsey. It turned out to be more like an execution than a genuflexion!

When she got back to her wheels, her master and mistress, trying hard to control their giggles, were disappearing through the door. She and R-T clutched each other's metal claws as the lovers passed into the house.

'Young love, isn't it grand!' said R-T oozing in his oils.

Navek and Peggy had a cup of hot cocoa by the fire. They sat on the sofa, hand-in-hand. A comfortable silence descended, which was broken only by an occasional spit from the fire. They felt no need to chatter. Theirs was the quiet communion of twin souls. The peace was absolute. Perfect. And there they sat until the fire flickered almost out. All that was left in the grate was a warm glow of a few dying embers.

'Time for bed,' said Navek. 'I'll just take another aspirin. I've got one of those damn headaches again. I wonder why I've been getting them ever since we got back to earth.'

He moved to the kitchen. Peggy heard the sound of water splashing in a glass. Returning, he scooped Peggy into his arms and mounted the stairs. Two peachy lamps glowed either side of the bed. Peggy was relieved and delighted to see how different the room looked. R-T and Gladys, upon learning what horrors the mistress had experienced in this room, had taken it upon themselves to redecorate. Gone was the huge four-poster that had dominated the boudoir. Banished too were the floral flounces and chintz curtains. A neat low modern bed sat where the old one had been. It had a headboard fashioned out of curved pieces of mirror. Everything in the room was the colour of creamy champagne. The fresh linen sheets trimmed with Broderie Anglaise were folded back on either side of the bed. The pillows, edged with more lace and delicate satin bows, had been expertly plumped by Gladys – an excellent housekeeper.

At the foot of the bed was a small octagonal mirror table fenced in by two elegant high-back chairs. On the table, waiting, stood two crystal glasses and a magnum of champagne – freshly chilled. The room's only contrasting colour was in the shape of a single red rose that stood in a fine porcelain vase on Peggy's new heart-shaped dressing table.

The whole ambiance of the new room was soothing and calming, in complete contrast to the horrors of their recent dreadful voyage. Peggy eased off her high-heeled slippers and let her toes luxuriate in the heavenly pile of the thick, creamy carpet. A nightgown of exquisite shantung lay on her side of the bed; while Navek's offering was a cream silk kimono.

Peg and Navek sat down at the table. He was about to

open the bottle of wine, when there was a metallic clank at the door.

'May we come in?' said the robots.

'Do,' the lovers chorused in unison.

R-T and Gladys shuffled into the room.

'We thought we'd just see if everything was OK before we retired to our staff flat in the cellar.'

'Why, it's wonderful,' enthused Peggy. 'I love your choice of colour for this room. And the bamboo embossed grass paper is simply divine. You have a marvellous camera for colours. And as for the antique light fittings, they're superb. Where did you get them?'

'R-T made a tour of the antique shops for those.'

'How did you settle on this subtle colour?' Peg enquired.

Gladys fussed unnecessarily. She looked down at her wheels. She seemed a mite uneasy. She poked R-T in the ribs with a metallic elbow.

'You tell them!' she said.

'It's like this,' rattled R-T, 'we'd noticed that you human men get the leaks when you love. We thought you'd probably get quite a lot of leaks in this room. We decorated in this shade, so that your leakings won't spoil our decor.'

'Good thinking Tinman. Sweet dreams. Go and switch your circuits off and have a restful night.'

The door banged. The servants disappeared.

Nevak popped the cork and the question . . .

'Will you marry me, darling?'

Peggy looked at him over the brimming glass of sparkling champagne. It seemed to Navek, her eyes held more sparkle than the bubbles; more promise than the pale honey-coloured liquid could ever have.

Her moist lips parted in a quiet 'Yes.'

Navek lifted his glass in a toast. The crystal chinked.

'To us,' he whispered, his eyes already undressing his bride-to-be.

Peggy had lost weight, but the new slimness suited her.

Her high cheekbones had become even more clearly defined. Her blonde hair shone like spun silk in the soft glow of the lamps. Her blue eyes were misty as she looked up at her fiancé, through a fringe of long feathery lashes. He could see the reflection of his own burning desire in her twin pools of passion.

Reaching out, he moved a strand of hair from across her face. He ran his forefinger down her temple, and around the smooth curve of her cheek.

Peggy reached up, catching his wrist in her grip. Turning his palm towards her, she planted a kiss on the flat surface. With her tongue, she traced along the groove that formed his long lifeline. Wrapping her lips around the base of his little finger, she sucked slowly up the side, until her moist lips closed over the tip. She kept her mouth still and, with her thumb and forefinger pressing either side of his hand, started to move the digit in and out of her fleshy orifice. Occasionally, he felt her teeth graze the skin. The sharp teeth were quickly withdrawn, giving way to the padded cushion of her lips. Peggy's eyes half closed, as she took the next finger in her mouth. She moved from one to the other, continuing her finger-suck along the line. Her spittle made a fine adornment for the upright poles. Soon, all four fingers were gleaming glistening pinnacles of pink. Peggy regarded Navek's long agile fingers with mounting pleasure. He had the sort of hands she loved – powerful but elegant. Peggy had always been turned on by a man's hands. They were the first thing she noticed in the men she was attracted to. After all, it was those deft members that would ultimately fondle her first; and be allowed to explore her most private of parts. She had never been able to understand why most men paid so little attention to their hands. Why they centred all their attentions on their cocks. But Navek was different. His hands were beautifully cared for. Nevertheless, manly.

He pulled his hand away from her mouth and ran his moist fingers down the vee of her dress.

'Come, let's try our new night attire,' he murmured.

He got up, moved to the bed, and dimmed the lights. Peggy sat and watched him as he began his unveiling ceremony. She stared boldly at his prominent bulge. He unbuttoned his cotton shirt and the garment whispered to the shag. He stood, legs apart, and unbuckled his belt. He was about to unzip his trousers when Peggy moved in. He felt her hot eager fingers fussing inside his waistband. Her hands moved down, over his stomach and played in his pubic plot.

'Not yet, Peggy,' he urged. 'I want to see you in your new gown. Feel your perfect body through that silky shift.'

Peg moved around to the other side of the bed. Not taking her eyes off Navek, she stripped to the music of his eyes, and when she had donned the garment, stood with her back to the soft glow of the antique lamps. She raised her arms to reveal the flowing lines of the beautifully-cut erotic chemise. She pivoted around and, through the gossamer peignoir, Navek glimpsed the shadowy shape of her lithe body. She stood facing him and their eyes locked in a look of love. They remained motionless for some time. Peggy broke the spell by taking a dive into the middle of the bed. Her gown rode up to show off her svelteness. She was aware of this randy revelation but did nothing to cover her pulchritudinous pussy.

Navek moved towards her. He bent his head to hers and his lips made the merest contact with hers. He was backing off again, when she slipped her tongue through her lips and beckoned him back. He settled himself beside her. They lay side-on, facing each other.

'You're very quiet,' said Peggy. 'Have you still got your raging headache?'

'No, it's gone now. Besides at a moment like this, how could I think of anything but you?'

'Oh, Navek,' she cried and moved sinuously towards him.

He held her back, placing his hands on her shoulders. Then, as if in slow motion, he pulled her gently to him. His mouth nuzzled against an earlobe and his tongue explored the outer edges of the perfect pink shell. His aural penetration lit a fire in her loins. The sensation of his sweet lappings made her realise that this new-found erogenous zone was as sensitive as her inner thigh.

Navek's hands dropped to her waist. He tugged the thin material of her nightie, pulling it taut over her breasts. The fabric moulded to her like a second skin. He could quite plainly see her pert aureoled nipples through the nifty shift. Like an arrow to its target, his mouth sped downwards and fastened upon the nearest nodule. Through the sheer weave of her gown, his lips tasted the nuttiness of her covered nodule. He chewed on it carefully; then, sucked ravenously. The cloth, sodden with saliva, became opaque. The sight of her rising sap forced him to denude her. He peeled the gown from her body. She lay there in all her lusciousness – waiting and willing to appease his lust. They were soon both unwrapped and unravelled – naked on their new couch.

Peggy's raw passion shattered the tranquil scene. She migrated south; straight to the heart of his sex. She went on a package tour of his Leaning Tower of Penis. She sauntered around his sex and gallivanted past his goolies. She lurked in his long and curlies; then took his swagman in her tuckerbag. She steered his boom into her oral locker. She was awash in an ocean of sexual sensations. Time seemed infinite. Navek gloried in her mouth. He felt her tongue moving stealthily over his large glistening knob. The point of her tongue lapped skilfully around the domed head. It ran down the side of his cock and playfully moistened the hairs at the base of his stalk. Before her inevitable ascent, Peggy nibbled at his scrotum. Then pushed her mouth nearer and took a ball, deep into her mouth. She sucked on the gobstopper, then moved to the other. She gave it the same sensual treatment before freeing it once more. Her face travelled up and she took his whole length in her throat. Her jaws moved artfully at the base of his cock.

'Stop, stop,' begged Navek. 'Don't milk me yet. I want to feel the warm walls of your well, pressing in on my prick.'

Peggy backed off reluctantly. She loved the feel of the shaft of stiff silk sliding in and out of her mouth. She wanted to suck him until he was dry and tender. But giving is the biggest part of loving. She gave the mighty member a last, lingering lick and then did as she was bid.

In a trice, Navek was upon her, forcing his legs between her own.

'My darling,' he moaned. 'I hope you won't think this silly but I've got a premonition. The thought of it makes me very horny. Something tells me that tonight you will conceive. Everything seems perfect. It's great that you're off the pill now.'

Peggy's lust-bubble burst. She thrust herself sharply forward.

Navek was sure he'd penetrated so deep, that he'd hurt her. He needn't have worried. However far he thrust, she sucked him in that bit further. The constricting walls of her cunt closed in on him. He could not contain himself. He proclaimed his love and lust with beautifully-mouthed expletives. Together, they blasted off into a climactic orbit of a lifetime. The sated lovers slept.

Much later that night, something stirred under the luxurious rich brocade bedcover. A chink of moonshine crept craftily through the curtains, casting a small shaft of light on the pillows. Peggy's blonde tousled hair spilled over the feathers. But there was nothing to be seen on the other lace pillow. The bedcovers next to Peggy twitched again. The girl slept on peacefully, as a green jelloid shape oozed out of the bed and on to the floor.

Minutes later, in the lean-to shed in the garden of the croft, the green monster sat in front of the radio.

'Ground control to Major Tom. Navek here . . .'

GENERAL FICTION

		Cyril Abraham	
Δ	042697114X	THE ONEDIN LINE: THE SHIPMASTER	80p
Δ	0426132661	THE ONEDIN LINE: THE IRON SHIPS	80p
Δ	042616184X	THE ONEDIN LINE: THE HIGH SEAS	80p
Δ	0426172671	THE ONEDIN LINE: THE TRADE WINDS	80p
Δ	0352304006	THE ONEDIN LINE: THE WHITE SHIPS	95p
		Spiro T. Agnew	
	0352302550	THE CANFIELD DECISION	£1.25*
		Lynne Reid Banks	
	0352302690	MY DARLING VILLAIN	85p
		T. G. Barclay	
	0352304251	A SOWER WENT FORTH	£1.95
		Michael J. Bird	
Δ	0352302747	THE APHRODITE INHERITANCE	85p
		Judy Blume	
	0352302712	FOREVER	75p*
		John Brason	
Δ	0352305355	SECRET ARMY: THE END OF THE LINE	75p
		Barbara Brett	
	0352303441	BETWEEN TWO ETERNITIES	75p*
		André Brink	
	0352305916	RUMOURS OF RAIN	£1.95
		Jeffrey Caine	
	0352302003	HEATHCLIFF	75p
	0352395168	THE COLD ROOM	85p
		Ramsey Campbell	
	0352304987	THE DOLL WHO ATE HIS MOTHER	95p*
	0352305398	THE FACE THAT MUST DIE	95p
	0352300647	DEMONS BY DAYLIGHT	95p*

BARBARA CARTLAND'S ANCIENT WISDOM SERIES

	Barbara Cartland	
0427004209	THE FORGOTTEN CITY	70p*
	L. Adams Beck	
0427004217	THE HOUSE OF FULFILMENT	70p*
	Marie Corelli	
0427004225	A ROMANCE OF TWO WORLDS	70p*
	Talbot Mundy	
0427004233	BLACK LIGHT	70p*
	L. Adams Beck	
0427004241	THE GARDEN OF VISION	70p*

† For sale in Britain and Ireland only.
* Not for sale in Canada. • Reissues.
Δ Film & T.V. tie-ins.

GENERAL FICTION

	ISBN	Author / Title	Price
Δ	0426187539	R. Chetwynd-Hayes **DOMINIQUE**	75p
	0352303514	Magda Chevak **SPLENDOUR IN THE DUST**	£1.50*
Δ	0352395621	Jackie Collins **THE STUD**	85p
	0352300701	**LOVEHEAD**	95p
	0352398663	**THE WORLD IS FULL OF DIVORCED WOMEN**	75p
Δ	0352398752	**THE WORLD IS FULL OF MARRIED MEN**	75p
	0426163796	Catherine Cookson **THE GARMENT**	95p
	0426163524	**HANNAH MASSEY**	95p
	0426163605	**SLINKY JANE**	95p
	0352302194	Tony Curtis **KID ANDREW CODY AND JULIE SPARROW**	95p*
	0352396113	Robertson Davies **FIFTH BUSINESS**	£1.25*
	0352395281	**THE MANTICORE**	£1.25*
	0352397748	**WORLD OF WONDERS**	£1.50*
	0352301880	D. G. Finlay **ONCE AROUND THE SUN**	95p
	0352304073	**THE EDGE OF TOMORROW**	£1.25
	0352304995	Norman Garbo **THE ARTIST**	£1.50*
	0352395273	Ken Grimwood **BREAKTHROUGH**	95p*
Δ	0352304979	Robert Grossbach **CALIFORNIA SUITE**	75p*
Δ	035230166X	**THE GOODBYE GIRL**	60p*
	0352304359	Elizabeth Forsythe Hailey **A WOMAN OF INDEPENDENT MEANS**	£1.25*
Δ	0352305142	Peter J. Hammond **SAPPHIRE AND STEEL**	75p
	0352301406	W. Harris **SALIVA**	60p
Δ	0352304030	William Johnston **KING**	£1.25*

† For sale in Britain and Ireland only.
* Not for sale in Canada. • Reissues.
Δ Film & T.V. tie-ins.

GENERAL FICTION

	0352303956	Heinz Konsalik **THE WAR BRIDE**	95p
	0427003210	**THE DAMNED OF THE TAIGA**	75p
	0352303883	**NATASHA**	95p
	0352304022	**THE CHANGED FACE**	95p
Δ	0352398981	Jeffrey Konvitz **THE SENTINEL**	70p*
	0352301643	Dean R. Koontz **NIGHT CHILLS**	85p*
	035230412X	Andrew Laurance **PREMONITIONS OF AN INHERITED MIND**	95p
	0352304154	Ellie Ling **THE FIRST SPLASH**	75p
	0352303328	Pat McGrath **DAYBREAK**	95p
Δ	0352396903	Lee Mackenzie **EMMERDALE FARM (No. 1)** **THE LEGACY**	70p
Δ	0352396296	**EMMERDALE FARM (No. 2)** **PRODIGAL'S PROGRESS**	70p
Δ	0352395974	**EMMERDALE FARM (No. 3)** **ALL THAT A MAN HAS . . .**	75p
Δ	0352301414	**EMMERDALE FARM (No. 4)** **LOVERS' MEETING**	70p
Δ	0352301422	**EMMERDALE FARM (No. 5)** **A SAD AND HAPPY SUMMER**	70p
Δ	0352302437	**EMMERDALE FARM (No. 6)** **A SENSE OF RESPONSIBILITY**	70p
Δ	0352303034	**EMMERDALE FARM (No. 7)** **NOTHING STAYS THE SAME**	75p
Δ	0352303344	**EMMERDALE FARM (No. 8)** **THE COUPLE AT DEMDYKE ROW**	75p
Δ	0352304103	**EMMERDALE FARM (No. 9)** **WHISPERS OF SCANDAL**	75p
Δ	0352304510	**EMMERDALE FARM (No. 10)** **SHADOWS FROM THE PAST**	75p
Δ	0352302569	**ANNIE SUGDEN'S COUNTRY DIARY** (illus)	£1.25
Δ	0352304340	**EARLY DAYS AT EMMERDALE FARM**	75p
Δ	0352304286	David Martin **MURDER AT THE WEDDING†**	95p
Δ	0352396164	Graham Masterton **THE MANITOU**	70p*
	0352395265	**THE DJINN**	75p*
	0352302178	**THE SPHINX**	75p*
	0352395982	**PLAGUE**	95p*
	0352396911	**A MILE BEFORE MORNING**	75p*

† For sale in Britain and Ireland only.
* Not for sale in Canada. • Reissues.
Δ Film & T.V. tie-ins.